OUT OF SILENCE

by

MARY SORRELL

HODDER AND STOUGHTON

Copyright © 1969 by Mary Sorrell
First printed 1969
SBN 340 10952 1

Printed in Great Britain for Hodder and Stoughton Limited,
St Paul's House, Warwick Lane, London, E.C.4, by
Hazell Watson & Viney Ltd, Aylesbury, Bucks

O Lord protect me;
Thy sea is so wide,
My boat is so small.
(Old Breton Fisherman's Prayer)

Remembering especially my gentle Mother whom I knew so little, and my wonderful Aunt who bequeathed so much to me without my even realising it – Blessud.

FOREWORD

THIS book is both an inspiration and an enchantment. It is first of all the story of a battle, the struggle of a very brave woman who was, and is, determined not to be defeated by an incurable cerebral illness. Most people, handicapped as she is, would have resigned themselves to invalidism. Mary Sorrell lives by herself, broadcasts, writes, paints, travels. She is not alone in her gallantry, there are other such stars shining in the darkness of our day and time, and many have written the story of their victory, but this story has something unusual about it, something that is hard to put into words. It is written by a woman who has refused to allow suffering to turn her inwards to self-absorption, but rather has given herself to be broken outward into sensitive awareness of every loveliness, great or small, that touches her. Whether it be the rough kindness of the London boys who came to her help when she was taken ill in the street, or the beauty of tiny sea-shells, her response, which can be one of near-ecstasy, is such that her reader seems to share it with her to the full. Sometimes, especially when she describes the beauty of Iceland, which is to her the land of heart's desire, she uses a sentence so vivid that one has the sense of being sharply pierced by some arrow from beyond time. This book has been written at great cost not to bring relief to the writer, but with the hope that it may bring encouragement to those who are fighting a battle that may be not unlike her own.

ELIZABETH GOUDGE

PREFACE

I SHOULD like to tell you how this book has been written. I think it may be of help to you in reading the following pages.

I doubt whether words issue from a writer's brain as steam issues from a boiling kettle. Naturally some people write more quickly than others. In my own case my brain seems to crawl over the surface of the paper, and my hand follows. My ear however is a reasonably good guide. Before assembling many of the sentences I have just had to try them out to hear if their rhythmical sound is correct. By that sound, even when the words are not actually musical, I can tell whether a phrase is good or not. Yet I cannot always be sure that any sentence is correct because my grammar so often lets me down.

A first cerebral haemorrhage on Christmas Day, 1954, deprived me of speaking, writing and reading. That is the reason why I find it hard to form words into phrases. I have tried to overcome the difficulty by the use of lexicons; Roget's *Thesaurus* and the *Oxford Dictionary* have proved a great help, but my most reliable guide, in fact my valuable friend, has been my home-made personal Word Book. Over a number of years I have collected words either from hearing or from reading them. I have immediately written them down and now I have literally hundreds of words at my finger-tips. They are in no specific order, so I have to glance down at the endless columns until I find the one word I am seeking. Many a time I have almost thrown my Word Book into the flames, thinking it would be of no more use. But I could not bear the idea of betraying one that had always been such a good helpmate. In this way then my vocabulary has been consistently enlarged. When I came to write this book however, I felt that it was extremely small, and my memory of the use of even these words plays tricks on me, as my grammar does.

Typing the script from longhand has been inordinately taxing on such a brain as mine, especially when I so dislike the medium. I made endless mistakes and continually lost my way. My damaged brain seemed to enjoy throwing dust into my eyes, but laughter, that precious gift from God, came to my aid.

I should like to thank the many friends who have helped me in one way or another during these intricate years. I know that I am privileged to have them: especially my consultant, who in 1966 became a Professor and whose gentle skill and encouragement never flag; and my Rector, whose spiritual advice and comfort are an infinite source of strength to me.

In conclusion I should mention the BBC and the producers concerned for so kindly allowing me to use passages from several talks I have broadcast.

PART ONE
1965

CHAPTER 1

THIS story is going to be the record of a voyage of discovery. The voyager is myself. The tale will be simply told, for words that were once my medium became strangled and muted. Then, very slowly, those words dripped hesitatingly, and more often than not could seldom be understood; words that refused to pour like rain upon the sweet earth, but seemed to drop like stones into a bottomless pit.

It began about eleven years ago, and at that time the sea of life was reasonably calm, though choppy. It varied from day to day. A voyage of discovery is always an event, whether it be of short duration or, as in my case, never ending. I had no idea at all that I would be going on a voyage, nor indeed where my ship would take me. But beside that floundering vessel, sailing alone and often near to sinking, I found Jesus Christ treading the blue-green waves, and ever ready to give me a helping hand when needed.

Eleven years ago I scarcely knew Him—only by name and not personally. I had been trying to find Him for some time, though rather diffidently, and life appeared quite full without Him—almost happy as I drifted along. My work as a journalist, in fact, a writer on art, was more or less a full-time job, and I loved it. Words were everything to me until the day came when the only word I could utter was my Christian name—Mary.

So gradually, and out of the silence of the heart this story will evolve. A still small voice suggested a book to me, but I was uncertain. A book would take so long, I thought; perhaps it would never be finished. Yet that voice still persisted and I listened to it.

Jesus said "I will never leave thee, nor forsake thee." Until I knew Him as my Friend I was not so sure.

It is not easy to begin a book, and I have chosen only the

last eleven years of my life because, to me, they are the most significant.

My aunt, with whom I lived for many years, was a maiden lady. She was devout and had a great influence on me. Every week I went to see my parents and my brother—especially my mother—and even when my aunt was extremely strict I was happier with her, although she did not always understand me, for I was a rebelious girl as well as being withdrawn. She was a Unitarian and I went to chapel with her every Sunday morning, but I did not become a member of the chapel. Somehow I never found what I sought there, and the sermons I heard seemed to me to be rather like intellectual addresses instead of plain statements telling me how I might find Jesus Christ.

Later in the book, you will read how, after many years of seeking, at last I found Him, and how much I owe to the church I have chosen . . . or maybe God chose it for me? It is not a Unitarian chapel but an Evangelical Anglican church, and I thank Him, for as Jesus said in St. Matthew's Gospel: "Where your treasure is, there will your heart be also." In the middle of a sermon I gave my heart to Jesus for His safe keeping.

In 1953, after a long illness, my aunt died. She lived to a ripe age, and suffered patiently and courageously. I never heard her complain, and to me, as I think of her now, she was one of the most Christ-like people I have ever known, although we often disagreed. One day, when I went into her room where she lay in bed, I saw that her eyes were closed, and her hands were clasped in prayer. I sat down silently and looked at her dear face, so peacefully calm; and still with her eyes closed she softly said: "My Father, I need Thee, be Thou my guide." Then she opened her cornflower-blue eyes and smiled at me. Eleven years have passed, but that moment is something I shall never forget. When I returned to London, and was thinking about it, I sat at my studio table and wrote the following poem:

IN REMEMBRANCE

My Father, I need Thee,
Be Thou my Guide:
Blest words she oft repeated
Flowed as half-dreamt dreams
At eventide.

Her fragile hands the air graced,
Moonlight pale were they;
A span of near one hundred years
Threaded their transparency.

And o'er her head
Aureoled,
With soft hair
Etheral rare,
Tendrils spun
Snow-breath fair;
Sweet surprise,
Shadowed memory
Ling'ring longlost
Within her eyes.

Blue-dimmed orb
'Neath hooded well
Culled her vision;
Heav'n she sought to tell
Lay
But a day's heart-beat
Away.

For one brief moment
Trembling on the brink of stars
Ripe earth a captive held her:
But the coverlet of joy
Her face awakened,
As love to love gave shelter.

My aunt's religious influence on me as a child languished when I grew to girlhood and it more or less deserted me when I became a student in London. Like many other students I tried various churches of different denominations but I did not find what I needed, which appeared simple enough to me. What I wanted was a vicar who would take me in hand, and who would make me sit up and think. I often felt like a sheep without a shepherd, or was it perhaps that I did not seek diligently enough? "Seek and ye shall find," Jesus said. But I took no heed.

In any case chapel-going was a thing of the past, and I was glad. Those services hardly ever touched me deeply, and only when I wandered into a beautiful church did I find something that profoundly stirred me — even to tears. Here, without realising it, I stood in the presence of God, and the sweetness of His house wrapped me around in silence and wonder. For wonder it certainly is, when an architect, out of the drawer of his mind is able to design a splendid church or cathedral to the glory of God. Would that I had thought of such matters earlier.

But I am not concentrating on earlier years that were both exhilarating and sad; nor on a broken marriage that was filled with nostalgic happiness and sorrows. My life began again as a journalist, but alas, without God. He would have helped me so much in those days as He does now. So I am going to try to unfold my memory over the last eleven pin-pointing years. A mesh of tangled thoughts, so long remembered, vacillate and slide through my being. My journey of discovery into the unknown may reveal hidden territories I had not hitherto explored, and I am ready.

CHAPTER 2

ELEVEN years ago I was a reasonably busy journalist, writing mostly about art for certain magazines. With all my heart I loved and revered words, and next to words I loved art. So I tried to combine the two, and to give meaning to words through art. It was not a profitable job, but then, art seldom is. I was happy in my chosen career, and I did not mind being poor. Food had never been important to me, and so long as I had sufficient to eat nothing else much mattered — or so I thought. During holidays I went to Leicester, my home town, to stay with my aunt who was by then bed-ridden. Sometimes in the summer I was able to paint a bit, for she had an extensive garden with many flowers growing in it, and there were tall trees in a field at the end. In the winter I would use a table in the attic, and write or paint there. I had always enjoyed the unexpected marvels of minor things. For instance, I vividly remember one particular cobweb. It hung in the corner of a glass outhouse, and the door was open. The morning dew on that sparkling cobweb made me swallow my tears. It was so perfect and so precious. I watched the spider weaving his web, more transient than laughter in the sunlight, and then I turned away.

Sometimes my aunt would talk to me about the future; but in old age the past is usually best recollected in tranquillity and so it was with her. As I said earlier she never complained and I used to wonder what she thought about.

One day, when I was sitting by the fireside, reading, she said suddenly:

"I shall leave you a small legacy when I die so that you can go abroad for a holiday. I know you'd like that wouldn't you?"

"Yes" I answered, surprised at what was in her mind. "Yes, I should very much. Thank you."

"And where would you go to?" continued my aunt.

For a moment I pondered. There was no point in pretending, and I could see that she was interested.

"Oh," I laughingly joked. "I'd go to Iceland again."

"Yes, I thought you would." And she smiled and said no more then.

One night my telephone rang, and I was told that my aunt had died. It was no use my going home at that hour of the night, so I went early the next morning. Soon after my arrival I went into my aunt's room and asked if I might be left alone with her for a few minutes. I felt a bit apprehensive since it was the first time I had encountered death. But I did not worry for her sake, for there she lay, like an old saint, her guileless eyes closed and her fragile hands crossed. She looked so tranquil and happy. And through my mind floated a few lines of Kingsley's song—the song she so often sang to me when I was a child:

> Be good, sweet maid, and let who will be clever;
> Do noble things, not dream them, all day long.

Tears flowed freely, because I knew that I would never hear her voice again. And all the time I kept hearing those words: "Be good, sweet maid, and let who will be clever." That was her message to me, I thought. I will try to honour it.

Looking through her papers I found her pocket-sized edition of *The Imitation of Christ* which was given to her in 1898. In the past I had glanced into it but, curiously, felt it overwhelming. Now I opened the book again and saw that many of the passages were underlined by herself. One that struck me particularly was this: "Fight like a good soldier: and if thou sometimes fall through frailty, take again greater strength than before, trusting in My more abundant grace: and take great heed of vain pleasing of thyself, and of pride."

I thought about this passage, knowing my own weaknesses, and instinctively I knew that the musty corridors of life would take a lot of time to clear. None the less, the seed had been sown, but would it take root?

Returning to my studio from the home I had known

always, which was now gone forever, I was trying to sort out many problems when a knock sounded on my door. On opening it I saw a doctor friend who had called to see how things were progressing after this sad upheaval. Usually we talked about religion and Shakespeare, arguing a great deal. This time, however, we talked only about religion. Catching me unawares he abruptly said . . .

"You've changed."

"In what way?" I enquired.

"It's not easy to define," he answered; "but something has happened to you spiritually."

He was right, but shyness overtook me and I said nothing. I felt that through the veil of my heart, and in so short a space of time those stems were beginning to grow branches, and by God's grace they might bear fruit and flourish.

Still the spiritual progress was slow, and I had no inclination to do much about it. By nature I had always been reserved, and this new awareness of Jesus Christ, instead of filling me with joy — gave me a kind of inner emptiness. The door of my heart remained closed. I had not read or heard of that beautiful verse in Revelation:

"Behold, I stand at the door, and knock: if any man hear my voice, and open the door, I will come into him, and will sup with him, and he with me."

No, I had not opened the door at all — not really; and those stems that were beginning to grow branches, and with which I was so thrilled, now seemingly began to wilt. As yet I had not wholly given myself to Jesus. My work as a journalist appeared more important to me, and I little realised that if I had asked Him, He would have helped me years ago. I persevered a great deal with my writing but not so much with God, though my aunt's death had given me a lot to think about, and at that time God was very much in my mind. Chapel-going had long been discarded, and I now shrank from speaking about Jesus Christ. It just never occurred to me to speak with Him. Nor did it once occur to me that I might find help by going to some church or by talking with a Vicar.

How wrong one can be in thinking one is self-sufficient without the protection of faith! Yet in real faith one can leap over a mountain, even perhaps move one "Faith that moveth mountains". As yet, obviously, I had not completely surrendered myself to God.

I would reach out and often seem nearly to touch the mysterious light that shone in the darkness but it continued to elude me.

On a side table littered with objects connected with writing, lay my aunt's shabby, well-worn Bible. Apart from reading it daily, I would pick it up and read a verse or two in passing. The tiny print of my own Bible which I had as a child, was now too small for me to see.

As I mentioned earlier, I loved words and the writing of them more than anything else in the world, but in chancing upon the words of Jesus Christ I ought to have loved Him and His words most of all. Had I realised the implications of His messages more thoroughly, and of their sweet chords of meaning, the spinning web of thoughts that now and then snapped, would have continued to weave indefinitely. A waking dream so often wafted me towards an invisible shore, and that distraction, lovely in itself, was treacherous to such a hasty person as me.

"Dreaming as usual," my aunt used to say. "You know you'll come down to earth with a bang one of these days." How right she was—but not in the way she anticipated, I imagine.

CHAPTER 3

THE legacy my aunt had spoken of duly arrived, and my thoughts turned towards Iceland. I had spent some weeks there before the war, and had made a number of acquaintances. Two friends and I had corresponded throughout the war, though intermittently.

From the very instant my feet touched her shores I loved her. I think you either love her at first glance and for always, or detest her. That largely depends upon your individual temperament, and whether you prefer a grand sweep of landscape to contemplate and walk into, or whether you would rather dance in sophisticated night clubs to soft music. If you enjoy the latter you will be sorry you ever went to Iceland because there are no hectic attractions. There is not a single public house nor a smart beauty parlour, nor indeed any shop worth mentioning except bookshops, and there you find every shop sells books published in many languages. Icelanders are avid readers, and according to the statistics of the population, in comparison with other countries, they sell more books than anywhere else in the world. And they are proud to boast about their low infant mortality rate, for it is the lowest on record. While our newspapers are filled with murder stories, in Iceland every murder is hushed up for at least six months and left in shame to the secrecy of criminology.

When I went to Reykjavik for the second time, in 1954, I knew that my aunt would be delighted. Although I had been there only once before, somehow I felt I belonged to that entrancing country. Not knowing when I should return home, I had first of all to fulfil several commissions such as articles on antiques as well as on contemporary art. I wrote to my Icelandic friends about my intended visit, and in the early hours of one morning the telephone rang and a voice enquired whether I could take a telegram. "It comes from the Arctic Circle," the voice commented. Dumbstruck with excitement I managed to listen to her message which more or less said, "Come and stay with us."

So naturally I went. But not as quickly as all that. This would be the first time I had ever been for a holiday on my own, and now I was going to the Arctic Circle and quite alone! As I am not materialistic, nor craving for money, the plotting of when to spend and when to save was not easy. As usual I did not seek the aid of Jesus Christ, especially when everything went swimmingly well. Now I know Him and pursue Him for much of the day, faltering frequently in my struggles for patient obedience.

My mind was a wanderer, sometimes fermenting within, and at other times blissfully savouring life without. This was an occasion for "blissfully savouring". Weeks ahead I booked my passage in the *Gullfoss*, tourist class because it was much cheaper: and on that Monday afternoon I remember how many of us stood on deck as we slowly sailed out of Leith docks. Rain unleashed itself in torrents.

The dormitory when at last I found it, was below deck. It was clean and comfortable, but when lying down you seemed almost to rest on top of the engine. Sixteen women slept in our dormitory and the equivalent number of men in the opposite one. For twenty pounds inclusive there and back, you could not expect a cabin. Food was excellent. Clamps were fitted to everything movable, and during two days of storms you were lucky if you managed to gulp a sip of your drink before slithering to the floor. Your nice cup of tea followed and swam around you. But what was that discomfort compared to the thrill of going back again to Iceland? As we paced the deck backwards and forwards on the Wednesday afternoon, our ship sailed high on white-crested waves. Glaciers shone gold-flecked in the Nordic sunlight. How aloof; how awe-inspiring they were. We steamed into the mountain-flanked harbour, and I saw my friends waving to me.

Had they altered during the years? Scarcely at all. After chattering a bit we were whisked away by car to another friend's house in Reykjavik, and were soon engulfed in drinking steaming coffee and eating slices of cream cake topped with banana rings, which is a speciality of Iceland. How good it was to be back again with my friends! Before long we were in the car and heading for home, a matter of fifteen miles or so. By their letters I guessed that they had built a new house, and there at last it stood, solitary on top of a hillock, at the foot of mountains. A natural waterfall became a stream and wandered through part of the uncultivated garden. How beautiful it all was! I took a soft breath and wondered whether I was dreaming, because at that period of my life I had a deep mistrust of happiness. Happiness of every kind, for sorrow kept creeping through my unruly being and I was unable to discover its source. Perhaps, unawares and without my thought, the branches of my inner stems were not growing as I had wished. They had not entirely wilted but I was busy on a multitude of quests, too busy to meditate more on Jesus. So the holiday progressed, and with exercise books ever ready beside me I made copious notes.

The friends I stayed with were kindness itself, as indeed were other Icelanders. My host, Halldór, whom I first met in Iceland before the war, is a writer of distinction. I had no idea, on my second visit in 1954, that he had become so famous. In 1955 he was awarded the Nobel Prize for Literature. He talked little about his work, and was devoted to his velvet-eyed wife, Audur, and their two small children. What fun we had together. Most mornings I travelled to Reykjavik by car or by bus and spent a great many hours there looking around, and thinking about articles I hoped to write on my return to London. Occasionally I had meals with friends in town, and then later Halldór or Audur, or both, would pick me up and drive back to Gljúfrasteinn, their mountain-side home. Often when walking in Reykjavik people stopped to greet me, and for a moment I could not identify their faces. This quickly became easy, for once having met anybody either at a party or in a shop, you were always meeting in the small capital of sixty thousand inhabitants. To go back to the west end of London is rather an anti-climax, for here you might walk for a whole life-time without coming across a single acquaintance.

Many Icelanders are not golden haired. A few have red hair and quite a lot have brown. As I strolled around I wondered . . . was it a Greek in the fourth century who discovered Iceland, or was it the Irish four hundred years later? In any case there was a strong influx of Irish element among the earliest settlers.

The go-ahead town of Reykjavik has, in parts, a Wild West aspect. It is a town of hills and narrow streets; and old timbered houses sit side by side with new concrete fabrications. Very modern architecture enlivens a district in a most extraordinary way, for each residence vies with the next in its inarticulate motley. (There are over two dozen busy architects in the capital.) I loved those Victorian lace curtains that ornamented sundry windows, and the pictorial accent added to the charm of the atmosphere. There are no roads anywhere except in the centre of the town, and one becomes used to showers of dust from moving vehicles, and to walking on ankle-breaking stones.

Each time I passed the Cathedral, in the centre of the town, it was locked. I wandered into the Roman Catholic church some distance away, and had a chat with a nun who was arranging flowers. Neither of us could speak the other's language but we managed just the same, and I did enjoy "the peace that passeth all understanding". As yet I could not quite understand, but I was getting nearer to the truth than I knew. In the church garden I looked at a tiny cemetery. It was for nuns who had died in their convent, and were buried in the garden.

Almost everything is within reach in Reykjavik. If not there are buses or you may prefer to ride on those irresistible ponies that thread nimbly through the crowded thoroughfare. There are no trains in Iceland, but there are plenty of motor cars; and aeroplanes will fly you to the north should you be hurried for time. The clock that dominates our English habits is practically invisible in Iceland, and even the Post Office did not possess one when I was last there! Finding your way about is much easier than shopping. There are three cinemas, a library and a National Theatre almost within the span of a few steps; and if you do not like walking, a bus will take you to the entrance of the University, which is a splendid building, both without and within.

I was astonished most of all by the quantities of paintings and sculpture everywhere. They abounded from the capital to the last solitary farm. Especially sculpture. You are always coming across it at the end of a street or in a square, and even in the most ordinary living-room. In Iceland, art is considered to be a necessity and not a luxury. And no wonder when we remember that the present generation of artists and sculptors are the very first in Iceland save for two or three nineteenth-century painters. Writers have their glorious tradition of *eddas* and *sagas* that are among the greatest works of mediæval literature. No artist there need starve in a garret, holding an umbrella beneath a battered skylight. He will be supported by the State, and this applies to writers and to musicians as well. Obviously Iceland is a paradise for them.

I spent a lot of time visiting artists and seeing their work. Yes, artists are truly fortunate people, and original art there is so cherished by the population that everyone seems to buy some. I am stressing this aspect of Iceland because in many countries the arts are left desolate as no one promotes their activities. Folk are not interested in reaping their benefit nor of cultivating the graces they give to the world.

CHAPTER 4

SAYING farewell to Halldór and Audur was not easy. My holiday had been so perfect, both sight-stimulating and exhilarating and in their company, just talking. As we stood by the *Gullfoss*, Audur took from her handbag a spray of wild forget-me-nots that she had earlier gathered from the moors. She pressed them on to my coat and their natural sticky substance held the flowers in place. For myself, a shadow deepened over the sparkling landscape, and I felt my heart being torn to pieces.

"*Blessud*," they called from the quayside, as I turned and waved. And our separate languages mingled in the same fond expression everywhere. "Bless you," I cried from the pulsating deck. "Bless you!"

Nothing of importance happened during the voyage to England. There were no storms, and I could hardly believe that I was going back home. But the exercise books in my case were bulging with ideas for articles, and I had high hopes of their acceptance. All went according to plan except that the leisurely life I had known for the last two months, and which is so much a part of Iceland, quickened with disastrous results. I thought of those bewitching days, and a kind of burning fever ignited my mind to such a degree, that in my affection for the subject I overworked. I did not mind how many hours I gave to my writing, even though the output was often negligible. Finding the right word and then developing it into a sentence seems to me rather like painting a picture, when the artist infuses his landscape with inventiveness and inspiration. There is no end to the felicity of words and their cascading sounds; and the deft touches they add, now and then, make an infinite difference to a burdensome sentence. With one word a languishing spirit may even be clothed in a rosy mist . . . for a while. My own spirit was beginning to droop with fatigue, so I imagined.

The empty shells of my words were not sufficient to satisfy me, despite the fact that I took unceasing trouble over their contents. But I did not take the trouble to read what Jesus said. His words were not shells, and He said . . .

"I am the good shepherd: the good shepherd giveth his life for the sheep. But he that is an hireling, and not the shepherd, whose own the sheep are not, seeth the wolf coming, and leaveth the sheep, and fleeth: and the wolf catcheth them, and scattereth the sheep. The hireling fleeth, because he is an hireling, and careth not for the sheep. I am the good shepherd, and know my sheep, and am known of mine. As the Father knoweth me, even so know I the Father: and I lay down my life for the sheep. And other sheep I have, which are not of this fold: them also I must bring, and they shall hear my voice; and there shall be one fold, and one shepherd."

It was nearing Christmas, and my commitments were almost finished. As a friend was coming to stay with me over the holiday I put away my work. Then a light form of influenza attacked me, but my doctor cured me. I was so anxious to be better for Christmas, and I remember making mince-pies, and scarcely knowing what I was doing. I felt so weak. Christmas morning came, bright and cold. My friend and I lunched out, and then we decided to go to Westminster Abbey to listen to the carols. After the service we returned home and were looking at Christmas gifts that were scattered about the studio, when the crisis happened, which was to change my life and outlook absolutely.

Unexpectedly, and without any warning, a most terrible pain struck one part of my brain. I felt as though it had been diagonally sliced right across, from one side to the other. I sat down and asked my friend whether she would be kind enough to find some pills, thinking this must be a severe headache. She did what I asked of her and I took some pills, but the pain continued. Not knowing that I was seriously ill, I went to bed and tried to make the best of what had been a happy Christmas Day. My friend ate her supper alone, as I could not face the delicious food I had prepared for the festive season. I took more pills and they had no effect on me, so in the morning she went next door to see my good friends, a medical consultant and his wife. It was Boxing Day, but he came scurrying round, and I remember little about the episode. Weeks later, when they came to see me in hospital, he told me that on that grim morning he had asked me: "Do you know who I am?" and I had mumbled —"I know your face but I don't know who you are."

Although he does not specialise in such disasters he knew at once that I had had a cerebral haemorrhage. After a telephone talk (though not in my hearing) my general practitioner arrived, and he told me not to worry because an ambulance would be calling for me in about five minutes! I had absolutely no idea what was the matter with me except that I felt horribly ill. The thought of packing some night clothes never occurred to me, and in any case the ambulance arrived in a jiffy.

When passing my work table I desperately clutched two books, both very dear to me. One was *The Imitation of Christ* which had belonged to my aunt, and the other was my Word Book. I then had no notion that I could not read.

The ambulance whisked me to hospital in minutes. There I lay on a stretcher, and I was questioned by a doctor. By then I was practically speechless, and the only intelligible word I could utter was "Mary"—my Christian name. It was ages before I could add my surname. One side of my brain had been injured, and I could not speak, write or read. I was neither young nor old, but youngish to have a cerebral haemorrhage.

When you are suddenly deprived of your faculties, you just cannot understand the strangeness of it all; at least, so it was with myself. It must have been about six months before I grasped the situation. Yet, however ill I felt, without knowing, an inner spirit impelled me to fight.

The first week in hospital was hazy to me, but the things I most remember were the nights. As soon as the ward was quiet my dreams began. They were silent dreams full of poignant memories. But as the night grew denser my dreams changed to waking nightmares that swiftly flashed across my vision, one after the other, and a fierce wheeling sensation turned round and round in my brain, never ceasing. I tried to remember where I lived, and although I clearly saw the interior of the studio, I could not fathom its whereabouts. I tried to remember the names of some of my friends, and where they lived, but everything seemed a chaotic muddle. One night I found myself trying to say "Our Father," and then I could go no further. "Our Father". I had no idea how the prayer continued. Soon I was to know that those two words were quite sufficient to pray to God. Now I could not remember, and I was full of fears.

The ward was extremely large, with some operation cases, quite different from my own. The ward sister was a darling, and so too was my almoner. How much they helped me, and the nurses as well! Luckily I usually saw the funny side, for everyone laughed at my odd speech when I tried to say something. Oh, how perplexing it was to pronounce the simplest word! When the trolley came round for breakfast I would point to what I wanted. I knew, but at any given moment I just could not say a syllable. The effort was unbelievably exhausting, and the wheeling brain never ceased wheeling. Yet something made me try to write a few words every day, and I bombarded my friends with so called "letters". I would write one or two lines, then lie back completely spent. Having gained a little strength, I would sit up in bed again and write more words and so it continued. Friends tell me they were the most fantastic letters, with made-up words and drawings to supply wordless spaces. Sometimes there would be two letters of a word and then dashes – hoping that the other person would know what I meant. By now I had my address book, and although I could not read the addresses I recognised many of them by sight. Each letter of the address was laboriously copied on to the envelope, but some, I was later told, looked most peculiar and my friends wondered how my letters had ever reached them because the addresses were so badly written!

Instead of lying down quietly, as I was told, I simply had to go on trying to write. I now realise that it was fear — fear that I might never be able to write again. Although speech was a Herculean task, it did not worry me in the same way, nor did I then seem to mind about not being able to read. But writing was my job.

I still have a pad on which I tried to write when I was first ill in hospital, and when I look at it now I can scarcely believe that I am endeavouring to write this book. Once I began to write the alphabet, and it ran thus: A H K N Y. That was my alphabet. I recall clearly the day when I asked a nurse if she would mind telephoning a certain sculptor friend and his wife. On the pad I see that I could not make her understand because I had drawn a statue on a plinth, with a telephone box and three pennies beside it! Eventually she comprehended for she found the name and address and wrote them down. She had also written the name and address of the hospital. There are many such pages on the pad. Somebody passing my bed usually came to the rescue and finished a word for me, or helped me to say the word I needed. On my part it was similar to miming, and people generally understood.

It was during the second week that a brain specialist came to see me. He sat on my bed and talked. Then he took a piece of paper, and on it he drew some triangles. He asked me what they were. Of course I recognised the shape but I could not say a word. I tried so hard to think but nothing came from that waste-land of memory. At long last I managed to stutter "pyramid", and we all laughed, for two other doctors had joined us. Next the specialist wrote the word TIMES and he asked me what it spelt. After much hesitation I said "times" correctly, and that utterance seemed really exciting. Then he reversed the letters, and I was asked to read the word, but it totally muddled me. I could not see that the letters were merely reversed.

Subsequently, the same specialist gave a lecture about my case. I know I was not a little anxious at being wheeled in bed into the lecture room full of white-coated doctors, but they were all so nice about it that my shyness diminished. The specialist showed me a gold dress-watch, and he asked me what it was. The morning was bad for me, for I could not pronounce "watch" at all though I knew the shape. Then I was asked the time. I knew the time exactly. It was twelve o'clock, but for the life of me I could not say so. Distractedly, and on a piece of paper, I wrote down 1–2, and the doctors knew that I knew the time!

The days passed and various tests were done on my brain and spine and so on. Some of them were interesting to watch, while others were less so. I still retain the painful memory of having a lumbar puncture, and of clutching the side of the bed for fear of shrieking. That test, I found out only recently, was to examine the fluid which surrounds the brain. Another day my dear ward sister sprang a surprise on me. She told me that I was going with a nurse, and by ambulance to a distant hospital for tests. I went, just as I was, and in my dressing-gown, and I had no thought of taking my handbag! How isolated that adventure is to me now; as clear as though it were yesterday. Sister and Nurse gripped an arm, one on either side, and guided me through labyrinthine corridors to the ambulance. They almost winged my legs over the ground, because they were far from steady, nor indeed was my brain.

In a dark room in this distant hospital I lay on a bed, while my head was massaged with a greasy substance. Over my messy hair a cage was fixed. Then the radiographer sat at a table before me, and tapping a queer machine she recorded my brain waves. I do not recall much about that, but curiously enough I remember being given an excellent meal afterwards, before we were driven back to our own hospital. There were other tests and X-rays. For instance, there was a saline drip in my right arm. My arm rested on a pillow and I had to keep the arm and myself perfectly still for four hours while the drip functioned. A cheerful foreign doctor, whom I had not seen before, came and talked to me, and realising that I could scarcely say a normal word, he just talked. That is something I shall never forget, for, as

Wordsworth wrote: "That best portion of a good man's life, his little, nameless, unremembered acts of kindness and of love." If I met that doctor now, after nine years, I would not recognise him, nor would he recognise me, but this one kindness to me remains engraved upon my mind.

Worst of all the tests was the one I called "Dante's Inferno". Its medical name is cerebral angiography. This is to outline the arteries of the brain. As I was not allowed to be given an anaesthetic (nor ever was I allowed this joy), I saw all that happened to me until the last minutes, when my eyes were bandaged. I will not describe the grim details, neither of what was inflicted upon me nor of what I saw. Suffice to say that an iridescent sentence and a pat from the surgeon as he removed the bandage filled me with happiness. After that ordeal I was carried on a stretcher back to the ward, and slept for most of the following two days. On waking I vaguely recollect a nurse who was bending over me.

Although I took *The Imitation of Christ* with me to the hospital and placed it on my locker, I found presently that I could not read it, nor any other book. Nor could I think about Jesus Christ, for then my brain was almost incapable of thinking. Hosts of friends called to see me, mostly from the art world, and they told me that I constantly mixed their names. I usually knew what folk said to me, but could not reply. A piece of a word might hang in mid-air, and a piteous struggle within me would try to pierce the cloud that shrouded my brain. It was no good, so I turned the situation into laughter.

Early one morning a nurse who was passing my bed, and who was interested in art, asked me who my favourite artist was. I had no doubt about that. It was Rembrandt, but say his name I could not. So the nurse gave me a string of names until she mentioned Rembrandt . . . Rembrandt . . . that was his name. Shall I ever forget that moment! But I could not pronounce his name at all, so we began with "Rem". Each time nurse came my way she would jokingly say, "What's his name?" And I would answer "Rem". It was not easy—even those three letters. Soon she added "brandt" and gradually I was able to say the entire name.

Another word I was most anxious to say was Reykjavik. During the first week in hospital a letter came from Iceland. I knew by the pretty stamp and by the handwriting on the envelope that it was from one of my Icelandic friends, but I could not read the letter, even though the contents were typewritten; so a house physician read it to me. Reykjavik was very near to my heart. I tried and tried to pronounce it, for it is a knotty word. As with Rembrandt, we split the syllables, and the joy of being able to pronounce Reykjavik once more was unsurpassable. Sentences baffled me completely, as indeed they baffle me still.

My gay ward sister, who was such a tonic to everyone, came late one morning to talk to me. She told me that I was going to be honoured by the visit of a great physician. I am ashamed to admit that it meant little to me. So many doctors came and went, and in a strange sort of way I was quite happy, except for the eternal wheel circling the brain, and the vagueness of everything.

It was two o'clock when I happened to glance down the ward. A stately greying-haired man wearing a long white coat was walking towards me. He stopped at the foot of my bed and peered at me over his crescent-shaped spectacles perched on the end of his nose. Then he said, "What have they done to you?" (meaning the variegated bruises on my neck and chest caused by that fearful test). And he smiled.

Instinctively I knew that here was the one person who would heal me. I had no doubt whatsoever, and silently I accepted the stranger. How can I thank him enough for his encouragement and kindness, and that of his team throughout the first five years?

After a thorough examination he sat beside me. "Now," he said, handing me a magazine, "I'm going to read this paragraph and I want you to correct me if I make a mistake." I listened intently, and then suddenly — did he really make a mistake? We both laughed. Of course he did. He read a bit more and again he slipped and I noticed it. He closed the book. "This time," he said, "I want you to pretend to be my secretary, and I'm going to dictate a letter, and you'll write it down." We began very slowly, and falteringly. I wrote about two lines. After that, the words trailed off and I could write no more. "I'm coming back in twenty minutes," said the Professor—and went away.

I was thinking about all this when he returned. He sat on a form beside my bed, and patiently listened to my strangled and incoherent words, and then he talked to me. Everything registered in that quivering abyss of mind, and some words that he said will haunt me until the end of my life. They were some of the most wonderful words that have ever been said to me, for they gave me hope when loneliness gnawed, and when inwardly I was on the brink of despair: "Some surgeons tell me that they could operate on your brain, but I prefer them not to. The brain, you see, is such a delicate instrument, and I prefer to leave yours to heal by itself. But I know that you *will* speak, and you *will* write, and you *will* read again. It may take three months or six months or a year, but I know you are going to do these things again." As he uttered those golden words he held my hand and then walked down the ward out of sight.

The shadows over my thoughts were now sunshine, and I felt as though I were in Elysium. That evening the Registrar came to me and asked me whether I would like to be moved into a single room, as one happened to be vacant. I was delighted, although I was perfectly all right in the big ward. Soon the little room had the touch of my studio because I had arranged cards around—reproductions of famous paintings that were sent me and so on. Once a paper boy came in and I bought an evening paper. But it was useless. I could not read, and the pages looked like glass to me. When the library trolley came with books, a lady brought me special books with reproductions in them. Those I could understand, and I often recognised the prints. I still wandered in and out of the large ward, and was glad to see patients there. One of them kindly allowed me to help her with early morning tea at some unearthly hour. We went into the ward pushing a hefty trolley. As we entered, she would shout in deep Cockney tones, "Oices — oices," while I handed cups of tea to patients. Her generous smile and voice captivated me. But the word "sugar" I could never say, so it was either "sugar" or "no sugar" from the patient as I approached with a cup.

I was sitting up in bed, trying to write, as usual, and was rather exhausted when a doctor came to see me on his routine check. I do not remember his exact words, but he gloomily told me that I would probably never be able to write again. At that utterance, and not being very diplomatic myself, I probably gulped with exasperation, and seem to remember muttering some demented sounds, more of anguish than of rage. Then I said — "But my Professor told me that I *would* write again, and nothing will prevent me — nothing."

As he left me I felt wretchedly upset, and I talked with the next-door patient in her bed. She cheered me up because she knew that usually I appeared to be a laughter-loving person. And she had more perception than the doctor. She quickly asked me to write something in her autograph album. So I brought out my Icelandic book with photographs in. It was given to me in Iceland, and once I had known the introduction by heart. The patient read out the quotation I needed (an old Icelandic proverb), and it ran thus: "Their mountains are their palaces and their poverty is their fortress." This I copied into the autograph album, making many mistakes, but the patient did not care. How thoughtful she was for others in her own illness! I have not forgotten her, even though faces and words habitually melt away, like tinted vapours.

In my hospital each patient is lent a New Testament. One day I opened mine at random. The print was good and I made out a word here and there. In that way I tried to read again, but oh, so slowly. It was such terribly hard work and seemed to hurt the brain more than anything else. And the wheeling sensation round and round my brain never ceased by day and in the sleepless nights. When I left hospital for the country, as a little remembrance, my precious ward sister gave me the New Testament I had found in my locker. By now it is thumbed and marked and much treasured. Months later, when I returned home, my gentle almoner came to see me, for she and my ward sister and I had become firm friends. She told me how she had noticed *The Imitation of Christ* on my locker, but did not mention the fact as I was too ill to think. Yet a whisper tells me that it was she who mentioned a church she liked; and in the fluttering confusion of my brain that chance remark registered itself.

CHAPTER 5

FROM the hospital I was driven to a small private convalescent home in Berkshire. It was essential to have quietude. But I was afraid—afraid of leaving the security of the hospital and of being among strangers. After saying farewell to the friends who kindly drove me there, I went upstairs to my pleasant bedroom and sat on the bed and wept. Mine seemed such a queer illness, and as yet I had no notion of what it was all about. I strove and strove to think, but a feeling of abandonment gripped me, and tears flowed swifter than before. In this unhappy state I heard a knock on my door, and the Matron entered. As I saw she noticed my tear-swollen eyes I turned to explain as best I could.

"Please," I said, "is it possible for me to see the Vicar? Does he live near?"

The Matron talked, and then she said she would do her best, adding, "It's pouring with rain outside so I'm not very hopeful."

I, too, heard the pelting rain, and felt pretty sure that no one would venture out in such weather. But Jesus Christ heard the call of this sorrowing soul, and within minutes a second knock sounded on my door, and in walked the rain-splashed Vicar. I had not moved from my seat on the edge of the bed, and he sat in a chair before me. In my efforts to talk I gulped and spluttered; but goodness from a holy man does miracles. Soon we knelt on the floor, and the Vicar prayed. I do not remember what he said, but silently and gratefully I accepted his words. He finished with the Lord's Prayer, and now and then I was able to join in.

I need not have worried about my uncommon speech, because people were very kind to me. Most of the patients in the home stayed from two to six weeks, and they rested and read and talked. Nevertheless I was conscious of my speech. I cannot describe the sound of it as it sounded to me. It was a mixture of stammering, hesitation and broken English, finally ending with exasperation at not being able to catch a word I desired. For weeks I was far too shy to try to speak much because everything took so long to say, and the sentences grew more and more entangled. Yet everyone seemed to know what I wanted to say, and again, as in the hospital, after the first word or two, somebody else finished the sentence for me! It caused lots of fun.

After breakfast I went to my room and tried to write letters to friends. I know now that they must have seemed the maddest letters, but at the time I did not realise it. To try to reawaken words from that enigmatic void . . . zig-zagging, scrawling words across a page . . . did it matter so long as they were words?

And where was Jesus? I had not forgotten Him, and I now knew that He was ever within reach and would come when I called Him. Yet somehow I had not become entirely reconciled to Him as I had hoped. Each Sunday I went to morning service in the little church on the green. I never opened any of the books in the pew, as I could hardly read. Nonetheless those services gave me immense comfort. Some-times the Vicar talked over my problems with me, and at other times I would go along and sit in the empty church for a while. It was peaceful there, and I felt a sense of God as I used to feel when, by chance, I walked into a cathedral or into an ancient church. But alas, I was restless, and as I could not read I went for long walks, nearly always alone.

Presently I had explored the countryside around, for I was out all day, apart from an enforced rest in the after-noon, and meals. From those solitary walks I learned a great deal about nature. Especially I loved hedges and ditches, and never tired of gazing into them. Each time I watched a spider dallying over its web, I thought of another cobweb, years ago . . . the one that hung in the corner of a glass roof in my old home. Only on this individual morning the sun-shine was pale instead of sparkling, and wild flowers drenched me in their fragrance.

A friend had given me a small sketch book, so I tried to

write a word as I walked along, or to draw something that caught my attention. Occasionally I made a sketch of the church on the green, or if rain persisted I stayed indoors and painted some flowers. As I look at those paintings in the folio beside me, I see how badly done they were. An adorable old horse grazing on the green was frequently fed by us, but I was not clever enough to draw him.

The convalescent home where I stayed had originally belonged to Ivor Novello. Everything about it was ideal. It stood in a charming garden surrounded by a stately wall. Here the composer's music room was built, and it had remained just as he had left it before he died, with his grand piano, piles of music, photographs and so on. We were allowed to wander in and out at will, and could visualise the musician at work. The spacious garden was all that one might wish for, with a limited assignment of convalescents of either sex perpetually coming and going. The home was meant for stage folk. I was the only convalescent who did not belong to the profession, so it was a complete change for me, and I enjoyed their chatter.

I constantly had to go backwards and forwards to the hospital to see the Professor, and to collect a new batch of tablets. Some were for the heart as that had been affected. One or both of my good friends next door fetched me in their car and took me to the hospital, and a sculptor friend drove me back to the country. How marvellously kind and considerate they were to me, as indeed were many other friends, too. How can I ever thank them for their kindness and generosity?

We were having tea one afternoon, and when listening to the conversation I heard somebody mention Iceland. Without thinking I said, "Oh, I've been to Iceland!" A sound from me gave people a shock, because I was still painfully shy at being so inarticulate. A patient asked me questions about Iceland then, and for a number of weeks after, and in that way he helped me not be so afraid of speaking. But the wheeling sensation persisted, just as though my head might roll off, and as from the beginning my balance continued erratic.

After several months I had to return to the hospital for three weeks. That time I took my paints with me, and each morning, after breakfast, I sat up in bed for about two hours, and painted flowers that were given to me. I wrote heaps of letters, badly written in all senses, but they were improving, and I could also speak a bit better. The many letters and cards I had from friends helped me tremendously, but I still had no idea what was the matter with me. No doctor had ever mentioned the word "stroke" to me.

From the hospital there was a further convalescence of two months. This time it was spent in Kent. It was high summer, and from that delightful cottage with its endearing occupant, one stepped into a lane bordered on either side with wild roses and honeysuckle. As before, I went for long solitary walks, taking my notebook with me, and gathering wild flowers to paint on my return.

At last it was time for me to go home.

A devoted old friend stayed with me for the first month, and after that the struggle really began in earnest. Shopping was an absolute nightmare. It was difficult to walk straight, and I must have appeared to an onlooker to have been drinking heavily! As for crossing the road, well, it was just a case of making myself step as briskly as possible to the other side . . . and hoping for the best! Worse than that was the terror of going into a shop and asking for what I wanted. I used to write everything down beforehand, but when I went into the shop, often I could not say the word I wanted, nor the sentence I had written. In desperation I would ask for something I did not need at all. All this was unbelievably frightening. With friends it did not matter, but among strangers it made me feel ridiculous.

Two or three months before I was ill I had finished a lengthy article about Icelandic artists, and when I was staying in the country the proofs arrived. To read consecutive sentences was beyond my power, so a friend kindly read the article to me. The pages looked unreal, but I recognised the many reproductions that went with the script. About the same time I had made extensive notes for two or more articles, and had even begun them. But would I be able to type again? I had been thinking about it for some time, but I had not dared to open my typewriter just in case. Now I knew that the moment had come. I laid my fingertips on the keys and very slowly typed my name . . . MARY SORRELL . . . tears of gratitude streamed down my cheeks. Then haltingly, and with endless mistakes, I typed my address. I closed the case and silently thanked God, for I knew that I would be able to type once more.

Eventually these articles were published, and a few others. But thinking was, and still is a torment, and it seems only possible to think intensively for a short while before feeling that I am going to fall over sideways and on to the floor!

CHAPTER 6

OUT of the ambiguous darkness in my brain I suddenly recollected my almoner speaking about a certain church. It was a moment in space — a special moment when God undid the crumbling doors of my soul, and I entered — unaccompanied and on a brief visit. He did not dismiss me, because He knew me to be impulsive as well as slow-moving. Now I was beginning to open my real heart to Him: the heart that one finds in the centre of quiet, and that gradually flowers like a gentle melody. Jesus said, "Behold, I stand at the door, and knock: if any man hear my voice, and open the door, I will come in to him, and will sup with him, and he with me." I was almost ready to invite Him in.

The church I had heard of was All Souls', in Langham Place just off Oxford Street. I had passed by many times without entering, but now it struck a dominant note in my scale of thoughts. I was more than anxious to go there, but as the exciting peak-tide of my writing had so violently ebbed away from me, I had reservations. I knew nothing about the church although I ought at least to have known something about its gracious architecture, and also of the Rector who filled his church to capacity. Going out in the evening was more than I could manage alone, so a kind lady doctor took me there one Sunday night. The church was packed, as I had anticipated, both upstairs and downstairs, and the inspired atmosphere I felt as I sat there filled me with more than astonishment. Everyone sang with passionate devoutness and voices of every kind gave free rein to their rusty human singing chords. It was impossible for me to read or sing, as my words trailed far behind the others; or when I did try to sing, the words were amazingly different from the printed page! But when I listened to the message of the Rector as he preached, his interpretations of the words of Jesus were what I had unknowingly sought. Jesus said,

"Come unto me, and I will give you rest." And in that split second I gave myself whole-heartedly to Him.

The Rector's sermon was simple and direct, and reached the heart. It was not an elaborate address. Here, without doubt, was a man of God.

Several months elapsed before I went again; then, one Sunday night I decided to go to church alone. About fifteen months had passed since the cerebral haemorrhage had shattered me, and as I sat in a corner seat of the church I grew more and more alarmed when such crowds of folk filled the pews. Would I be able to exist throughout the service without falling over, I pondered? The wheeling sensation circling the brain still harried me, until I feared I might scream. But all went well outwardly, and afterwards Jesus guided my faltering footsteps through the porch and down the stone steps and to the bus stop. "I will never leave thee nor forsake thee," He had said. What a splendid sermon I had heard! Although I could remember only a crumb, that particle raised my illuminated faith to the sky.

Lots of sermons begin with promise and continue with interminable tedium and to many of us, as children, they were bugbears, and equally, to some adults they still are. I think that generally depends upon the preacher, and of course upon his message – as a cake depends upon its ingredients. Often it has been, and still is, difficult to have faith, yet I should have known better than to have any doubts. I grew despondent, but as ever, with the comfort and understanding of the Rector, who by then knew my weaknesses, a calmer spirit prevailed over my irrationality. And there were compensations I had never dreamed of. Most of all, the long seeking had ended. "Our Father" . . . I thought of that night in the ward when I could go no further.

And now I am going to describe what Sunday means to me, and why I love it so much.

It was never long enough for me, and there were a thousand things to do. There always are. In this hectic world there is never any time – *never any time*. We work like wizards for six days, and on the seventh day, for many of us, it is just the same. I know, for I used to do likewise, and Sunday became one of the most energetic days of the week. It seemed also to be one of the most abysmally dull. In some respects my Sunday is still busy, but with a difference because I go to church on that day, and even though it is the most early-to-rise day of the week, I love it best of all. Besides that, I have found a haven of peace in church, and even if I treasure this peace in my own home, it is not quite the same – at least, not to me.

Sometimes on a Sunday evening I pass a West End cinema on my way to church; and I look at the long queue waiting to be admitted to the film. I look also at the extortionate prices of the seats, because where I am going all the seats are free. The cinema I frequently pass has dazzling lights that attract the mass, and I notice the names of various film stars that appear in big letters on the hoardings. And honestly I cannot help sympathising with the queue of people because I know how weary their feet are – just a shuffle at a time before they even reach the box office. My feet were weary, too, and they still are. But in the inner cloister of my being where I silently tread, and where I sit on a hard pew instead of a plush seat, I find strength in listening to the words of our Lord. Those words are not evanescent. They continue forever, like an unbroken thread; and when I come away from church a trusting emotion sustains me, and I feel as though I am awakening after an unnatural and bewildering sleep.

After all, the cinema is not the only place that is packed with people on a Sunday, and if I do not start early enough for my church, either morning or evening, I have sometimes found myself among the overflow, and being gently shepherded to the church rooms next door, for there the service is relayed. It is an amazing phenomenon, but it happens to be true; and people of every age and nationality attend. Some of my friends try to persuade me that our clergy make a difference to the worshippers, but I am sure they do not. We are human, and we cannot help being swayed by the

Rector's eloquence, and that of his curates, but if we are really in earnest we also listen through their messages to God.

Are not most of us caught in the web of life, one way and another? Some nets catch the heart while others catch the head, but Jesus told us to love our God with all our hearts and minds. And I think that any preacher with a message, and who shows us the way to find God has much more than imaginative eloquence. I call that an earthly miracle. The Rector definitely showed me how to find God, and in a flash I was ready. For years I had been floating about like a piece of wet seaweed, and now, in His sweet graciousness He anchored me to Himself. It was up to me not to float away again.

As I live some distance away from All Souls', I go either in the morning or evening, but not to both services. Usually when I walk away I look back—not in anger but in joyfulness. For as I expect there are crowds, literally crowds of folk streaming down the steps of the portico homeward bound for the Sunday dinners or suppers. It is a sight to melt your heart. For myself I prefer the quiet evening walk from the bus stop to the church. I pass that cinema and I see those huge placards with glamorous stars on them. They look so life-like that they almost appear real. And yet, in a sense I scarcely notice them because a few yards away I see the church's spire, and sometimes it is floodlit. And looking higher still, I often see a myriad of heavenly golden stars twinkling at me from the dark sapphire sky. My footsteps unerringly tread on solid concrete, but as I walk up the steps of the portico I always seem to hear that inner Voice saying, "Come unto me, all ye that labour and are heavy laden, and I will give you rest."

By now it will be clear how devoted I am to the church I have chosen, and how my spiritual life has changed. It may, alas, not always display itself with dignity and common sense, for shy people are reticent, and in my own case impulsive, too – an odd mixture! Believing myself to be a

45

Christian, I know that I am a sinner, but through my repentance God, in His infinite mercy, has forgiven me.

In my fragile ship, sailing alone, the journey often seems unendurable. We have had to avoid those relentless rocks— my craft and I—and try to weather the black storms that blow up. Our course over the everlasting sea of life is one of whirlwinds and of soft ruffling breezes; and a puff from the wrong direction sends us adrift. Even though I cannot see Jesus I know He is there, but sometimes I am too busy to depend on His guidance. So I must try again—and again, and I will try eternally.

On my voyage of discovery I came across a surgeon who very much wanted to hypnotise me. He was an expert in the profession, and was anxious to help me to try to get better. When I mentioned the matter to the Professor he was much against my being hypnotised, so I was glad because it did not appeal to me either. Then someone kindly suggested a professional faith healer, but that also was not greeted with particular enthusiasm, for I preferred to continue in the same lone way. Well, not exactly alone. There was the Professor and his team of doctors who looked after my medical needs, and there was the Rector who fulfilled my spiritual needs. And there were friends I had known long before I was ill; and new friends who joined this nomadic circle. Truly they were all wonderful, and here I would so like to add "thank you a thousand times, and thank you again."

About the middle of 1956 I went to see the Rector for the first time. Then my speech was extremely bad, but he knew something about my illness, and realised its difficulties. After a talk he asked me whether I would like to take Holy Communion in the church I so much love. "Bring one or two friends along as well," he said. So my ward sister and my almoner went with me, and the Rector officiated in the side chapel. The church was locked during the little service so that we would not be disturbed. Before starting he opened my Prayer Book half way through, knowing that it was going to be a nervous ordeal for me, for I still could scarcely read, nor could my brain often follow the beautiful service.

This particular Holy Communion had gigantic implications for myself, for it was the beginning of a new life in Jesus Christ. As we all knelt saying part of the General Confession, I said practically nothing for I was unable to follow; but I listened as best I could . . . "Have mercy upon us, most merciful Father; For Thy Son our Lord Jesus Christ's sake, Forgive us all that is past; And grant that we may ever hereafter Serve and please Thee in newness of life, To the honour and glory of Thy Name; Through Jesus Christ our Lord. Amen."

That service is one of the most cherished hours of my life.

During the second year of this illness—that was in 1956—the Professor took me to see the consultant psychiatrist in the hospital. The psychiatrist was extremely kind and he advised me to give up writing altogether just for one year, to give my brain a rest. Yet somehow I felt that if I did give up trying to write, even for a single year, I would never be able to write again. The psychiatrist named various pleasant occupations in the art world that I might learn to do, and they sounded absorbing, but they were not meant for me—or so I thought. After trying to speak well, and growing more and more exasperated because I could not say what I wished, at last I murmured "*damn*" and apologised. The psychiatrist laughed and said, "It's enough to make anyone say 'damn'." Now go home, and I'll have a talk with the Professor." And that was the last I heard from either of them regarding my doing handicrafts. Obviously it was better to leave this patient to go on with her writing, which she did.

In 1957 and 1958 I wrote a few short stories and they took months to write. As I was not in circulation in the art world I wrote about inanimate friends around the studio, a photograph I happened to see in a shop window, and so on. I wrote them for the sheer delight of writing, so there was no time limit, and I had no editor to please. I also wrote two small articles for my church magazine.

Sometimes I went to the West End to look at an Exhibition. The pictures seemed to swim round the walls, and I really saw nothing that I could describe. All the same it was delightful to be in the galleries again. I appeared normal to an onlooker who knew nothing about me, but if somebody spoke to me about the paintings it was horribly difficult to answer, and the more people questioned me the worse my brain became. When walking I tried to look straight ahead because turning to the left or right among crowds put me off my balance.

Again, and unnoticed, a miracle was taking place. The wheeling sensation spinning round my brain without interruption was becoming less noticeable, so that eventually I did not heed it at all. I cannot say how long that irksome, devilish and intangible symptom tussled with me, but the marvellous thing is that it no longer worries me any more. Crowds harass me, and I have been to no evening parties of any kind for many years. My only outing of an evening has been to church, when streets are usually deserted, and I am fairly sure of not being jostled over.

Dates of months and years now mean a lot more to me than ever before, as an indication of medical progress. I remember that when a physician gave a lecture to some doctors about my case, and I was there, he had snippets from two articles of mine. He also questioned me. The lecture was technical, and I understood little save the fact that for the first time I learned that I was expected to advance only slowly after the original six months!

CHAPTER 7

My dear old friend of eighty-two and I were sitting down talking. She had recently come to stay with me, as she does each year. The time was April, 1958. I was not used to loud knocks on the front door, and when I opened it I saw, standing before me, my Icelandic friend, Halldór! He was in London for a few hours to see his publishers. Halldór was ever unpredictable, but the news he offered me was almost too good to be true. He and Audur wanted me to have a holiday in Iceland, and to go in June, if possible, and also to stay with them for as long as I liked. "Everything will be arranged," he said, "and the whole visit from beginning to end, will be our gift." All that I had to do would be to follow the instructions that would later be sent. By then I thought I must be day-dreaming. Would the Professor allow me to go, I wondered? The three of us talked it over, and my old friend said, "Of course you must go, dear," and Halldór agreed. So I hurried to the hospital and asked the permission of the Professor. He said, "You go and forget everything and everybody." Well I tried to do just that—in moderation.

I had two months in which to prepare for the visit, but as I was going by plane I had to consider weight. I was never one to travel light, but this time I had to obey orders. My good friends next door lent me a pair of scales and on this I weighed every single item I intended to take with me, not necessarily only clothes. My Wellington boots I carried, hoping that the weighing office clerks would let me through without payment for these ungainly articles, and they kindly enough waved them aside.

This was the first time I had flown to Iceland, and incidentally it was my first flight ever. The two previous journeys had been made by sea. We left London Airport in the late afternoon at 5 p.m., and we arrived in Iceland about four to five hours later. As we soared higher and higher I could scarcely believe my eyes when we looked down on to banks of clouds and specks of land. Was that really England below us? (On my return flight I had no doubts whatever because the luxurious trees and the gorgeous green landscapes I saw as we flew above assured me that this was truly England.) After settling down, dinner was served, and that was a new experience for me, and enjoyable, too. Our Viking was a fine and comfortable aeroplane, and for most of the journey we flew across the sea, and saw no land. When, later on, I recognised those lofty glaciers I knew that we were nearing Iceland. Soon we caught glimpses of the outskirts of Reykjavik, and before long our plane touched down at our northern destination.

Audur, together with Sigga and Duna (their two young daughters) were waiting for me. Halldór had an appointment which prevented him from joining them. After passing through the customs office we quickly jumped into the jeep, for it was pouring with rain, and muddy underfoot. Audur drove through the now familiar meandering road, where friendly cows grazed or sauntered on and off the green verges, and a thin ribbon of steam told us of a small hot spring nearby. Scattered about was a handful of farmhouses, and on either side of the valley mountains of various shapes and sizes stood guard in their austere grandeur. When I recall that landscape it comes freshly to my mind, as it did when I was wandering elsewhere in Iceland. The colours of the mountains were ever-changing, and their pendant shadows sometimes had a metallic quality; and at other times, a supernatural light flushed the sky. It all seemed impalpable and unearthly. As a child I had always loved mountains, and I then probably thought of them as romantic and solitary. My feelings for them are just the same but with added dimensions now of immensity and mystery, and not least beatitude.

Driving along and chattering as though we had met only yesterday, we saw Gljúfrasteinn, isolated in the distance. A rising slope places the house higher than anything else in the valley, and the name of the house translated means Rock of the Glen. Gljúfrasteinn, built in concrete with double windows, needs to be as solid as a rock, for it is buffeted on all sides, and I have never heard such formidable winds lashing the walls from the moors. In fact, on one occasion, when we returned home, we had to crawl on all fours from the car to the front door, in case we were blown over!

On the evening I arrived from England the steady downpour gradually relented, and our jeep bumped noisily over masses of stones and across the narrow bridge that spans the flowing stream, and then turning slightly to the right, we drove up a short wide drive to the house. The hour was getting late, but in Iceland during the summer months there are two hours of darkness only, and I do not remember ever seeing electric lights illuminating the rooms. "You're going to have the same room," said Audur. "Your room," she added.

One wall was lined with books of every description and language, and there was a fresh writing table with drawers on either side. I had a bedside lamp on a small table, and an idyllic view from the window, overlooking mountains and moors, while the same stream gurgled by – as Tennyson wrote, "forever". We had so much to talk about over our midnight supper, and apart from the illness that had stricken me since my last visit to them, I had also my beloved Friend, Jesus Christ. That was something new – very new . . . for in those spheres I had never aired my views about religion. Tentatively I told Audur something about it, but it was too late to talk much longer. The day had been enormous for me – almost incredible, and now words had deserted me.

I am not writing about Halldór Laxness, nor the fact that Icelanders regard him as their finest prose writer since the great historian Snorri Sturlson, of the thirteenth century. It so happens that Halldór and his wife are old friends of mine, so naturally their names run in and out of the pages about Iceland.

My holiday of six weeks or so was perhaps the most untroubled one I have ever experienced. For one thing the weather was glorious, while in England we read that there was no summer at all—only rain and cold winds. We lay in the garden for much of the day, content to do nothing except to bask in the warm sunshine, and to enjoy a landscape of unsurpassed beauty. The large garden consisted of both cultivated and wild patches; of hillocks and plains, and of course the waterfall and the stream that passed through their land. Sometimes I sat on a rock dabbling my feet in the cool water, or dubiously crossing a shallow part in order to reach the opposite bank. On this trip notebooks were taboo, for my holiday was to give me strength, and not to tax my brain. So I did absolutely nothing and tried to obey those concerned. My cup of happiness seemed to fill every day, and laziness was part of the plan.

Sunshine in Iceland is one of God's most cherished gifts, for at the sight of a glimpse of sun Icelanders down tools, whenever possible, and take advantage of that heavenly glow. We were never indoors except for meals, and even Halldór relaxed. Not that we were always at home. One weekend Halldór decided to drive us to Akureyri, a day's journey by car, or an hour's flight north from Reykjavik. We left home at 8 a.m. and arrived at Akureyri about ten o'clock at night. Halldór's white Buick was sumptuous and we glided easily along. Fortunately he is an excellent driver: some of the roads were so narrow that a shave could have sent us down a ravine. Much of the road was unmade (like most Icelandic roads) and was straggled with big stones, and bumps we received often nearly hurled us through the car's hood! That was definitely not the car's fault, nor that of the driver. Never to be forgotten was the stark magnificence of that background of mountains. It was rather like a frieze etching the sky from one end of the earth to the other. Somehow it was uncanny and illusory. And closeted in the valleys we noticed motionless fjords drowsing there, while glaciers loomed in the distance, and barren fields of lava stretched along those pinched roads.

When we arrived at Akureyri, tired out with travelling,

there indeed was a sight that I am never likely to forget. I was just retiring to bed after our late meal, when I looked through the window, and before me, blazing in all its fiery glory, shone the Midnight Sun, that celestial miracle which is well nigh impossible to describe.

I liked Akureyri much better than Reykjavik. It was smaller, with even fewer shops. The new church, built on high ground, dominated the town, and you had to walk up innumerable steps to reach the entrance. It was breathlessly hard work, and you seemed as though you were strengthened from within for your dauntless climb to heaven! I remember that the first thing I did on entering the church was to sit down and regain my breath. Then I noticed pieces of sculpture made by Icelandic sculptors, but as my memory has faded I recall no more about the church save the gaunt outside image. The new hospital there impressed me immensely. Its situation was perfect, and patients overlooked a sylvan lake bordered by mountains. As I needed a little medical attention (and was soon cured) we were in time for tea, and were shown over parts of the hospital, including the huge kitchens. Our cakes came straight from the oven, and they were delicious.

One morning, when my friends went visiting, I had preferred to sit by the lakeside, enjoying the scenery. Before long a company of schoolchildren joined me, and they offered me sweets and hilarious fun. In return I had nothing to offer them except laughter as we tried to say words in each other's language. Presently they cycled away, returning quickly with more playmates and more sweets!

Driving home was eventful because a gale blew up, and its force was such that roads were swamped in rivulets, and we missed an avalanche by a fraction of a second. By the time we reached Gljúfrasteinn the sun shone and tearing raindrops changed to a mere drizzle; and to cap everything a rainbow jewelled the sky. Our white car, however, had become piebald in mud.

A week prior to my flight back to England I really did walk inside the Cathedral at Reykjavik. I was having lunch with a friend in town when I happened to mention the Cathedral and how it always appeared to be locked whenever I tried the door. So she offered to go with me, and together we tried the main door. As usual it was locked. We peered about and stalked all round, and unexpectedly we heard a typewriter from within the church. Obviously there must be a door somewhere, we thought. And there was a side door, but no one would have noticed it unless they were accustomed to using it. We hammered and hammered until the door was opened by a pleasant and surprised looking gentleman. My Icelandic friend explained our situation and we were shown inside. Although I knew scarcely any Icelandic, nor the gentleman English, we soon readily conversed or mimed—or both. First we were shown the special silver that is used in Holy Communion, and then we were each given a Communion wafer to bring home. Mine came back to England with me, for in my church we use bits of bread, and I had never before seen Communion wafers. We were fortunate in that the organist was practising, and so we sat in a pew and listened to him; but alas, I quite forgot to look at the inside of the Cathedral!

The Icelandic church is either Lutheran or Catholic, and as many people live in outlying farmhouses or in their summerhouses (as they are called), the church-going population is not large. Driving inland one sees a gaily painted thimble-like church often set in the middle of a field. Once we passed the tiniest church in Iceland. It was charming, resembling a big doll's house, and it was built of turf and driftwood. On top of the turf stood a diminutive cross, and behind the moors, and subtly contrasted, was a chain of everlasting mountains.

Sometimes we talked about religion, and periodically I would tell my friends how God has changed my life. As a youth Halldór became very religious, and he lived in a French monastery in the Duchy of Luxembourg, where, for a year, he learned how to pray. Then he studied in London with the Jesuits, and later he visited Rome, Lourdes and other Catholic centres, but eventually decided that a reli-

gious life was not his vocation. I remember his study, lined
with books, where often we discussed all sorts of problems.
Intoxicated by the scenery I would stand idly gazing
through the wide window that spanned the length of one
wall, and on to that telescopic view of near mountains and
moors. We seldom talked about illness, and as my friends
were so kind and understanding I tried my best to overcome
the trials that this illness had given me.

All things come to an end – so they say – and my holiday
had been an Elysium. I flew home suntanned and refreshed,
with places and faces for ever blooming in my heart.

CHAPTER 8

At the beginning of 1959 there came a crucial point. I feared that I was going to be turned out of my studio, and as I was unable to look around for somewhere else to live, life became alarming. Although I had faith, I had not as much faith as I believed, and grew depressed and downhearted. The slightest query blanketed my mind, and wisdom was never my best subject. "Seek and ye shall find; knock, and it shall be opened unto you." I sought and I knocked, without much hope, I fear. Yet Jesus Christ heard my plea and He caused still another miracle to happen, and of a sort I had not anticipated. Two friends who had been students with me decided to buy the studio as an investment, and they generously said that they would allow me to stay on as their tenant, and for the same low rent. As was the custom, I would continue to deal with inside repairs, and my friends would look after the studio outside. For that gesture I am intensely grateful, and a gigantic load was lifted from my mind.

The studio is laced with a treasure of memories; of luminous colour and of silent recollection. And here and there a light touch of my hand toys with a piece of Icelandic sculpture or I may glance on the big reproductions of that country that were given to me, and which are pinned to parts of the walls. Oh, there are so many possessions within this framework of illusions, and often I think of the words of Turandot: "The colour of eyes are but the colour of tears."

Painting and sculpture had ever been delectable to me, apart from a means of earning money by writing about them. I had never considered myself to be a critic, but one who was related to art, and who practically always wrote about the work she admired. As I was unable to think quickly, nor to train my reasoning where time had left a gap, I seriously began to try to paint as a project of making a living. I had no particular gift, but the ancient art of China had ever appealed to me. Two Chinese artists, whose work captivated me, were friends of mine. Gingerly I mentioned the matter to them, and with beaming smiles they unhesitatingly gave me some rice paper from Hongkong, Chinese brushes and a stick of Chinese ink. From childhood I had possessed a paint box of one sort or another, and now I was destined to begin.

Painting on rice paper is not easy. In fact, I would go so far as to say that it is the most difficult of all paper to paint on because it is so thin, with the fineness of tissue paper. I watched my Chinese friends paint, and was absolutely fascinated by the quicksilver turns and twists of their brushes, and by their skill and facility. I adored their soothing colour schemes in a low key, as melodious and fragrant as a whiff of pure air. Watching them merrily painting was to me at once dazzling and breathtaking. I had no doubts whatsoever in knowing what section of art could influence me. Very few artists are entirely original, and one generally senses influences in the best of them. I realised the truth of this especially when I wrote about art, but luckily no stigma is attached to it. So, unashamed, I dug deep into the evocative magnetism of Chinese flower paintings, and later on, of landscape.

To start with, I used scraps of paper I found in my folio, mostly using my Chinese brushes, though sometimes I painted with sable brushes that were presented to me. These bristles were both tender and firm, but they did not give me the rhythmic grace of my Chinese brushes, nor the harmonious unity I felt in employing them. In due course I discarded the sable ones and have since seldom painted with them.

Trying to paint from scratch on unfamiliar material such as rice paper is deceptive, to say the least. So also is speech when one has to begin all over again. Listening to other folk pronouncing words or sentences, and then trying to utter them yourself, is rather like being almost suffocated before the rescuer arrives, liberating you and your words — or so it seems to me. In painting, sometimes it "comes off" and you are overjoyed with the result, and vice versa. And it was just the same with my speech, and frequently it still is. Full of nervous energy I am ready to camouflage a dreaded sentence. Then nothing happens, and I am as inarticulate as a fish. But here I am not concerned with speech, but mainly about art.

As I stumbled along from scratch painting on my rice paper, pandemonium incessantly broke loose. My brushes would either be too wet or too dry. More often than not they were saturated, and a blob of water spread indefinitely over a page, and my flower disappeared from sight! Spasmodically my brush asserted itself and took over my reasoning, with the consequence that a picture emerged and I was tolerably pleased. The rice paper challenged me, as that still small voice incited me to try to write this book.

In a collection of sayings I found the following words from the *Talmud* . . .

"God wants the heart."

Towards the end of 1959 my paintings slowly improved, although my thoughts were apt to dilly-dally along the labyrinthine channels of fantasy. In one sense that was good fallow since in Chinese paintings artists always paint from memory. They study and contemplate nature, and later recapture the essence of what they beheld. As I have never been very observant this was a new training for me. In a black mood of despondency I would suddenly ask my Chinese friends whether they would kindly give me a lesson, for without doubt I was in a quandary. Sure enough they soon came, brushes and rice paper in hand, and together they examined my paintings, giving me advice, and setting me afresh on the right track. Their advice did not amount to talkative lectures. They merely illustrated on rice paper what other people would have said in words, and I understood. To a certain extent this fluent method transformed my life. It released those creaking hinges of repression, and when I read the following verses by W. H. Davies, it expresses a morsel of what I felt:

> *I hear leaves drinking rain,*
> *I hear rich leaves on top*
> *Giving the poor beneath*
> *Drop after drop.*

What a lovely verse to think about!

Most of all I had a fondness for painting roses. They obsessed me, as later did mountains and mirages of water. But, however much I studied leaves and their formations, I found them complicated and troublesome. As yet my hand was not sufficiently subtle to twist the brush in its musical performance. Be that as it may I managed to paint trees and mountains in landscape, together or separately, and I am perfectly sure that in ruminating over Icelandic scenery, it usually colours my rice paper. Fitfully a bird will perch on a branch, or a swarm of bees dot the sky, but human beings do not appear in my solitary landscapes.

Towards the end of high summer in August 1960, I went to see the Rector to show him my paintings. Some were now mounted, and I carried them in a large folio. I remember that the day was cloudless and very warm. After a little talk I opened my folio on the floor in order that we might look at the paintings from above. I suggested to the Rector that if he knelt down he would see them from a better perspective and that it was quite customary for artists to do this instead of propping the pictures around a room. So laughingly we scanned the paintings in this way.

In the hall, when we shook hands and said good-bye, I felt a sharp pain cross my head. It was momentary but unaccustomed. Then when the Rector opened the door I felt another sharp pain as I zig-zagged across the pavement, and I thought something was wrong. "Are you all right, Mary?" he asked.

"Yes, thank you," I gaily said. But I was not so sure. As I walked up the street with my folio under one arm the Rector again called after me, but I assured him that all was well, so he closed the door, and I went on walking. I was making for the Underground, and was beginning to feel unwell. My head seemed queer, and I was conscious that people behind were perhaps imagining me to be tipsy. Subsequently I stopped and changed the folio to the other arm. Then I zig-zagged to the station, and as it was a Saturday afternoon no teashops were open, so I could not sit down and rest. By now I was very ill but had no knowledge of it. Inside the entrance of the station I clung to an iron gate, hoping that I would not fall.

Surprisingly enough, although it was a half holiday no one was about. Trying faintly to attract someone's attention from the street, I spied three youths standing at the corner, so I waved and called, and they came towards me. I explained that I thought I must be ill and could they please possibly find something for me to sit on? They were so good, those Teddy Boys . . . and tears flood my eyes as I think of them. They found three potato boxes from somewhere and on them I thankfully sank down.

What happened next is somewhat confusing. I know that I was violently sick as two policemen approached. I apologised for the mess, and one policeman told me not to worry, and that I should go on being sick if necessary. It didn't matter, he said. The other policeman cleared away passers by who were now congregating in the station's entrance. After that two ambulance men appeared. They told me that I was being taken to a hospital in the vicinity, and on hearing that report I was extremely upset. I remember begging a policeman to hang on to my folio which was more important to me than anything else, and he promised to do so. Then the two ambulance men took hold of my arms, and on getting up from the potato boxes I found that I could not walk.

On being lifted from the ambulance to a stretcher on wheels, I was taken through the out-patients' department and into a private room. By now my brain was getting hazy, yet I recall showing a doctor the telephone numbers in my diary. He read them out and I named the friends to whom he said he would kindly telephone. The policeman who came with me brought in my folio, and a few hours later another policeman rang the bell of my good friends next door, asking whether they knew anyone by the name of Mary Sorrell. They received a shock, especially as we had spoken that same afternoon. They were told what had happened and where I was; also that I had now had another cerebral haemorrhage.

CHAPTER 9

THE doctor who attended me on that Saturday evening gave me three different injections, and I recollect no more until the following morning. I was still lying on the stretcher in my day clothes when I was wheeled into a lift and before long into the bay of a big hospital ward. There a nurse undressed me and I fell asleep. At that time no one told me why I was there, and I felt too ill to care. In the evening when I awoke, I was delighted to see a friend, and she had brought me some night clothes and toilet articles. During the succeeding week I had not the faintest notion that I was semi-conscious, but I seemed to wake when friends visited me, and was able to join in their conversation and laughter. My speech appeared not to have deteriorated any more, and I thought I would soon be going home. Little did I know.

Apart from recognising friends who came to see me, the first thing I remember of regaining consciousness was of a nurse giving me a blanket bath, and presently, of feeding me. I asked her the time and how long I had been there. "A week," she said. A week! That flabbergasted me. Then I turned over in bed, and the dizziness – oh, the dizziness – it is impossible to describe it. Floor and everything around throbbed and jumped up to meet me, and I thought I was going to fall over the side of the bed. Gradually I became more conscious of my surroundings, but the slightest movement was agonising; not with physical pain, but with the turbulence in my brain. So far I had not been allowed out of bed, and I did not know what was in store for me. As I was trying to find my bearings a doctor came along and stood beside me. To my great surprise he said, "You've had a very severe little stroke," and he continued to talk.

This was the first time the word "stroke" had ever been mentioned in my hearing – certainly not in my own hospital or elsewhere. It agitated and somehow frightened me. After the doctor left me I was eventually allowed to try my legs, and the result was catastrophic! Had it not been for the arm of a nurse I would have succumbed to the floor with giddiness. My legs were not paralysed but my brain was so capricious and inadequate that this second cerebral haemorrhage had affected my legs. The gyrating wheel that had tormented me for so long was not a symptom of this stroke, and in due course I realised that I must try to conquer a new horror.

My Rector came to see me and helped me in so many ways, and after a three weeks' holiday he was surprised to see me there and still in the same place.

Like all patients who have been confined to bed for days, their first request is for the bathroom. And so it was for myself. I was wheeled to the bathroom and given a real bath. Never shall I forget that bath, nor the oscillations in it; nor indeed getting out of the tub (with the help of two nurses) and standing still without bumping my head against the wall. These small pleasures, such as taking a bath, help to make each day a joy for a sick patient. I adored my bath, especially when I was able to look after myself, but I did not breathe a word of the difficulties of the operation inside the bath and out of it.

Day by day I tried to walk, firstly with the help of a nurse. As she said, when we rolled down the ward to the bathroom – we looked for all the world like two drunken sailors! I was so dizzy that my arm in hers made us both reel. My ambition was to walk alone and to reach the bathroom door, some distance away, before falling over. Then I would push open the door and recline on a chair on the other side. To achieve this feat I used to hold on to bedsides as I passed, and then I clung to a lengthy table. On my last lap there was nothing at all to cling to so I walked those few yards alone.

In this ward most were operation cases, and no one had the same malady as mine while I was there. Of course, I know there are thousands of patients with my complaint who are much worse than I am, and if any read this book I do hope that it may be of help to them in some way. The second cerebral haemorrhage seemed to afflict me with a terrifying lucidity, and at times I felt I was "a border case". In a curious way, perhaps known only to myself, fathomless stimulation attacked me, and no one knew the spiritual anguish I suffered. A curate, attached to the hospital, used to come and talk with me, and his kindness and humour were a source of happiness to me.

How wonderful are humour and compassion. Indeed, to my mind they are two of God's most precious gifts.

Once or twice the curate gave me Holy Communion in bed and I was grateful for this refuge, for in my particular case my brain seemed to be blown in all directions, and like an apocalyptic wind it was seething underneath with despair. And the smouldering ghosts again appeared as laughter.

As my legs grew stronger I staggered down three flights of stairs to the hospital shop on the ground floor. There I did some shopping for patients as well as for myself. A nurse always knew my destination and I did not leave the ward without permission. Those stone steps were hard work, because my head was still inclined to swim; so I would rest half way and look through a window to the green trees beyond. Returning to the ward I frequently took the lift, but subsequently I managed the stairs both up and down, gasping at the top, hoping that no one would notice.

As before, my friends were inordinately generous in coming to see me, and in this hospital visitors were allowed at any time, as well as the usual hours. The consultant who looked after my case was away on holiday until my last week there, when he came to see me twice on his rounds. The humorous smile he gave me as we talked about my episode in the street, and of being picked up by those nice Teddy Boys, was a tonic. "And remember," he said, "don't camouflage your feelings any more."

An old lady of eighty who was in the next bed to mine, and who was very ill, is now safely in Heaven. We became good friends, and we shared half-secrets over our laughter. I often think about her; and her daughter and granddaughter come each year to tea, when we talk about those unforgettable hours. A jolly home sister who came round the ward each day used to stop at my bed to look at the many picture postcards that were sent to me. They were often amusing, and some were colourful reproductions of famous paintings. I propped them up on the bed-table in front of me. I would apologise for my untidy bed, as it always seemed to me, compared with other beds, but she never minded she said, so long as patients were happy.

Six weeks elapsed and I was now ready to leave for a private convalescent home in Kent. My good solicitor, who deals with so many varied problems that are not his concern, now arranged for a Red Cross car to take me there, and in a trance-like state I went. A doctor suggested that I ought to use a walking stick when out so as to give me confidence. I was reluctant and felt embarrassed, but I soon grew accustomed to using it. The actual giddiness had gone, but an inexplicable ineptitude seized the brain and made me cautious, as though I were falling over, especially when tired or writing too many letters.

The convalescent home had once been a manor house, and it stood elegantly in well-groomed gardens. Sweet-smelling lavender bordered some of the flower beds, and among other fine trees, a willow graced one of the lawns. Willow trees are my favourites, and I made a number of drawings of this one but I did not paint much. My room overlooked a picturesque landscape, and a stream complete with swans and ducks beckoned me to the window. Most evenings after tea, I wandered by the stream and fed those fascinating birds who waddled up to the wire fence to catch each scrap.

On opening a gate at the end of one path you were confronted by the village church and its churchyard. It reminded me of Stanley Spencer's churchyard paintings: they were so lifelike, and I used to stand there and think of him as I knew him, and of his work. On Sunday mornings I went to the service and felt better and spiritually renewed. During my stay at the convalescent home I met two people and the three of us became good friends, but one of them has now returned to her native land of Australia, and I doubt whether we shall ever meet again. The other friend kindly helped me to correct some of the bad English in the first part of this book.

Our sleepy village was just right for convalescents. It had one main street and minor off-turnings. There were buses for those who wanted to go further afield, but I was content to stay put, apart from ambling about the countryside. My stick was of the greatest comfort, and without doubt, as the doctor advised, it gave me moral support.

The shortest way to the village was to wander past the church, and often I looked inside and sat down for a while. Somehow I did not find what I was seeking there. Alas, I could not find Jesus, nor did I have the strength to pray to Him with all my heart. An inconceivable issue had arisen within myself which temporarily clouded the horizon, and to which I could find no answer. Eventually my own Rector restored my flagging belief, and a flicker of faith that so easily waned in my distress now became strong once more; and I knew for certain that Jesus loved me. Did He not say, "If ye shall ask anything in my name, I will do it"? In my own weakness, as though it were suspended in a void, I had forsaken the truth of His words . . . "If ye shall ask anything in my name, I will do it."

CHAPTER 10

HOME again, and my studio as welcoming as ever! The last time I left home, with my folio under my arm, had been on that venturesome Saturday afternoon, from which I did not return for years — or so it seemed to me. Everything looked about the same, and my dear friends next door had filled a vase with flowers from their garden. Home . . . its very smile lights up your own face, and the leaves of time unfold as you open your case to unpack. I did just that, and in the unfolding of time it took ages and ages to assemble my thoughts. What was the next move, I pondered? To go to my own hospital and to see familiar faces that for so long had been part of my life? I had missed them.

There was much to talk about with my new consultant, although he was not exactly new to me for on and off he had attended me from the beginning of this illness, so we were not strangers. How grateful I am to him; more grateful than I can ever express!

People so often poke fun at patients and their doctors. Newspapers are full of such stories, but I deplore it, and here I would like to say that a sick patient needs not only medical attention, but understanding as well in both patient and doctor so as to achieve the best results. Humour plays a big part on both sides, and to be able to laugh together is surely a large portion of the cure.

I had decided to concentrate on painting for a while, and my consultant encouraged me to do this. Periodically I took my folio of work to show him, and it was about time for me to show him the new paintings, when I resolved to try to write this book, and we talked about that instead. I had been working intensely hard trying to manipulate my Chinese brushes on rice paper, and although that was difficult enough I found that it did not affect my brain in the same way as did writing good sentences. Reading had ever perplexed me, more than anything else, and for nearly two years it played havoc with my eyesight. When I tried to read, the words appeared to jump all over the page, or else my eyes seemed double sighted. Now my vision is normal, with the aid of glasses to read; but I must admit that I read curious words that, when I glance again, never reach the printed page, or for that matter, do not exist at all.

About the middle of 1961 I went to a tea party. Sitting next to me was a man, and when I was introduced to him he said: "Mary Sorrell—whatever has happened to you?" It was a freak coincidence, as he remembered our once meeting, yet I did not remember him at all. He knew, too, my writings on art, and wondered why I had suddenly vanished into thin air. I said I had been to Iceland, but in my excitement of talking about that beloved land, my sentences grew confused, and I had to explain why. I had no earthly idea that this acquaintance was attached to the BBC. When he pressed me to say more he presently said, "Don't tell me any more about Iceland. What you tell me about this illness is fascinating. Will you broadcast for us?" At that invitation I was dumbfounded, and felt I must think about it. Making many excuses, and never having seen a tape-recorder, I did not realise that words and sentences could be erased, and the record cut almost to pieces and put together again. The BBC administrator explained that I need not bother about my sentences being grammatically correct; for in my belief, they had lamentably fallen from good to bad, and my good English is something that has never returned.

So I talked it over with my consultant, and he agreed that I should do the broadcast. I wrote the script, and as I did not have to worry about my grammatical sentences and so forth, it was much easier than writing this book. A BBC producer read the talk, and he discarded some of the rambling sentences, and pulled the script together.

Giving a talk "live" would have been too devastating for me. For two hours with a stop watch we rehearsed and recorded before making the final record. The talk was to last fifteen minutes, and never shall I forget that palpitating morning. I did not wish to listen to the record afterwards, and preferred to wait until the date of the broadcast. In due course in the *Radio Times* I saw that the producer had called the talk "Out of Silence". That pleased me, because I knew that I could not have thought of such a title myself. A few days later I happened to meet him in the street. I asked his opinion of the final record and he said, "Well, it wasn't as bad as I expected!" At that observation I tried to shrink into nothingness.

Wednesday arrived, and shaking with timorousness, I turned on my transistor radio, and sat down to listen to myself broadcast. Did those almost incomprehensible years belong to me? And did my faith try to sustain me then as it tries to do now? The record ended and I leaned back and sighed with relief, and was soon lost in thought. But not for long. The telephone began to ring in my studio, as well as at Broadcasting House, and letters came to me from all over the country via the BBC. How generous unknown people were in listening to my talk, and in writing! I replied to every letter, and as each listener asked me quantities of questions my mail took me a month to reply. It was a privilege on my part to be given such an opportunity, and I concentrated on the problems of the individual's illness, similar to my own, and in some cases far worse. A letter was mostly a four-page epistle, because it had to be done thoroughly. In my letters I tried to suggest ideas that might be of help to the sufferer, though naturally nothing to do with medical aid.

After this talk I recorded others, and one of the talks I gave was about a book that much impressed me, *The Way of a Pilgrim*, translated from Russian. This book not only drew me nearer to God; it also helped me to read as I lay in bed before turning out my lamp. Fortunately it was easy to digest and the story enthralled me, so much so that after two or three months I had read the whole book. Although it is a simple book to read, I could only struggle through a few sentences at a time and then put the book down until the next night. I remember how much I looked forward to going to bed so that I might read a bit more about that old Russian pilgrim and his journeys. The words that most deeply penetrated my mind were those of the little prayer the pilgrim loved so dearly, and which was frequently quoted . . . "Lord Jesus Christ, have mercy on me."

Recently I have read the book again, and I have enjoyed it a thousand times over now that I can read better, and my brain can take a trifle more. Maybe I was meant to read the book a second time, because its echo is still crystal clear in my mind. The idea of being a pilgrim on life's adventurous highway appealed to me. In a sense it is analogous to my own experience of sailing alone in my small ship on a boundless sea. However, there are important differences. On the roads or in the streets one may encounter fellow pilgrims wearing ordinary clothes, and carrying baskets or brief-cases in their hands, or the traditional knapsacks on their backs, while in the sea lane of life, where traffic is less thronged, one meets more rarely another lonely voyager.

Once, engrossed in day-dreams, which is not an unusual state with me, I happened to glance through the window of a bus, and noticed a most unfamiliar sight. There, ambling along, his knapsack on his back, and a crook in his hand, went the incarnation of my Russian Pilgrim. As the bus slowly passed by him I gazed at this tall, bent figure, with his shabby black cassock, and his shoes tied with string. Where was he making for, I wondered, and did he, like that Pilgrim centuries ago, keep bread and salt in his knapsack, and a Bible in his breast pocket? That I shall never know.

However, to pilgrims the world over, the path to God is not a simple one to tread. It is thorny and you get buffeted and crushed. Your eyes grow dim with tears and you cannot see. But once you have set your heart on God nothing really deters you — nothing at all.

On my lonely voyage I have discovered pilgrims of every nationality and creed. And like myself, who once groped in the darkness, and whose eyes were not yet opened, they found that ultimately the well-spring of inspiration in all things is Jesus Christ. Without Him, to my humble person, life seems meaningless. Now it is full of surprises, and those inner resources given to us by Our Father in Heaven, help me to combat the persistent weaknesses of speakers who often do not listen before they speak. How involved one becomes with words, forgetting to probe one's way carefully, as restless rhythms that wreck a whispering passage of colour.

CHAPTER 11

A YEARNING caught me in my painting — possibly about two years ago. It was no good . . . again I could not prevail on my brushes to do what I most longed for, and that was to paint a single rose. To some readers that may sound ridiculous, but those who know the pure simplicity of Chinese brushwork, with its gracefully flowing lines, will understand my purport. A tension arose between the painting and myself, and I threw away one piece of rice paper after another. When I thought I had finished the painting, I added another touch — and spoiled it. The dilemma was so acute that I was beginning to wonder whether I would ever be able to paint the evanescent tints of the rose I visualised, a rose that was not academic but real all the same, with nature's interpreter that transfigures reality.

Obviously I would never discover that special rose on earth, and my imagination was not sufficiently skilful to conjure up the spiritual rose on rice paper. My eyes knew perfectly well the anatomy of a rose, but my thoughtful heart was desolate and forlorn; and the more I struggled with my Chinese brushes, the more stubborn and inflexible the picture became. Somehow everything I painted looked either timid or harsh, and nothing of any merit satisfied me. The whirl of introspections took me through the ways and byways of recollections, and I went on seeking without inspiration. Quotations, apart from the Bible, descended upon me in a frenzy, and one of my favourites kept knocking on my brain:

> *A durable fire*
> *In the mind ever burning,*
> *Never sick, never dead, never cold,*
> *From itself never turning.*

Like roses, the colours in my paint box had the most

ravishing names such as viridian, indigo, aquamarine, vermilion and so on, and they glimmered with ideals. For my part I learned how to sob soundlessly, and how to weep with unshed tears that were veiled in smiles. "Jesus, where are You?" I almost cried. For in that immense silence of haplessness the world seemed suddenly to escape from my slumberless brain, and it waved a wand of enchantment around my distractions. Shrouded in phosphorescence I stood on the brink of an abyss, waiting for something . . . waiting . . .

Any creative artist has, I feel sure, experienced such an emotion. An invisible obstacle emerges, and you become bewildered in your disbelief. This intangible substance was undermining the outer shell of my deeper self. And the deeper self was becoming more and more involved, divining no solution. Formed out of nothingness, and like a bubble that evaporates, the torn shreds resultantly fade leaving behind a blue mist of unsmiling moods. In this dejected state I came across the following quotation from *Isis Unveiled*: "I tell you, whosoever you be that wish to explore the depths of Nature, if what ye seek is not found inside yourself you will never find it outside. O man, know thyself, for in thee is hidden the treasure of treasures."

With this tricky illness one invariably becomes obsessed by anxiety even when the worry has no real consequence. In the anxiety of my trying to paint, the rose was fully manifested in the exaggeration, the poor quality and the opaqueness of the painting. It was similar, and for that matter it is still similar to a word or to a phrase; a rose or a branch of roses, one has to string them together, and in my case I am hazier than before. I may hesitate for a word or a sentence, turning the pages of my Word Book backwards and forwards in order to find the exact expression and its imaginative content. And in so doing I may perhaps allow my mind to slide lingeringly over one word or one sentence for an hour or even for a day. This to me is a labour of love, and well worth the labour and the love.

In between sessions of trying to paint the special rose with

73

its hallowed overtones, I painted landscapes. My memories were nearly always of Icelandic scenery, without actually painting any particular place; and I thought of mountains and fjords, and skies that in Iceland seem to roll from one end of the earth to the other. Lulled in sunset they were intoxicating, but I did not attempt to paint them. And in my solitary landscapes, sometimes and absurdly I gilded the world in a riot of vivid colour schemes; then, after a brief survey of the pictures, I liked to brood on the remoter space of infinity, and what might lie beyond.

But my special rose problem still remained unsolved.

At the same time of the year, namely in the early winter of 1962, when my rose paintings were becoming a problem to me, I went to see my consultant on one of my frequent visits. Under my arm was a heavy folio of paintings which I had brought to show him. Spreading them around and all over his desk, he studied them carefully, and presently he decided that he liked best the roses. He had no idea that they were giving me so much trouble, and I did not tell him. But when I went home I looked at my rice paper, and instead of taking a nice new piece I sat down and doodled on an envelope. Then I took a scruffy bit of paper and dipped my Chinese brush in water. I began painting the heart of a deepish pink rose. Next I added the petals that grew paler as they opened. Then I painted a stem that was touched with thorns, and from the stem sprang a spray of leaves. In my excitement I scarcely knew what I was doing. It was over in a flash, for Chinese painting must be done quickly, and in this instance I was quick. And oh, joy of joys, as I looked down on to my torn scrap of rice paper, I saw the sweetest pink rose I had been praying for for so long. In a half-dream I had watched it being painted, and was part of it; and the blown petals, which for weeks I had tried to achieve, had in this painting almost floated into soft pink nothingness. I had not noticed that in the happiness of these moments my own thoughts had opened and flowered. I gazed reverently at the gentle pink rose – the rose without any perfume; and my eyes were glazed with tears.

That rose was not for sale, but I painted others and some of them were sold. One morning my Chinese friends called to drive me with my folio to meet a publisher, whose business was some distance away. The publisher was interested in several of the paintings and to my astonishment, he chose one for publication, and asked me whether I could paint a companion within a week's time. The picture he chose was of a spray of pink roses, the one not yet created must be of red roses. This was an agonising situation, and as I sat in my studio painting one spray of red roses after another, then tearing them up, I thought I would never be able to do what was requested of me. But I managed it. The framer kindly and hurriedly mounted the red roses and, although they were not ready within a week, the publisher gave me a few days' grace.

On April 30th 1963 the two prints appeared and I was able to give my consultant a copy of each, for I was due to see him that morning. And just by chance I was broadcasting a talk that very afternoon, and the talk had been recorded earlier. So the two incidents led to evocative results, both shadowy and heart lifting. As I sat in the studio that afternoon, listening to myself broadcasting, I offered a little prayer of thankfulness to the One who has befriended me whenever I have stretched out my hand to Him.

Since I began my voyage of discovery on the high seas of life, my craft and I have battled with endless tribulations as well as basking in the light of jewelled rainbows. It has been a breathless and incomprehensible experience, and one that will continue on land after my book is finished, and so long as I live under God's radiant dome of Heaven.

These evocative thoughts plucked me away from the paintings I was writing about. Let us then return to the two reproductions of those roses. The publisher appeared to like them, but said nothing. However, he asked me whether I could paint two single roses; one yellow and one red. I thanked him and said "Yes," my nerves inwardly jangling.

These roses were as agonising to paint as the previous ones, for again they were a commission, and I was not a trained artist. So usually it was a hit or miss on my part. Two colours I found, were almost unattainable. They were red and green. But throwing out one piece of rice paper after another, I was faintly compensated with a few versions of the roses, and they were duly mounted and accepted by the publisher. Rice paper easily becomes crumpled and shabby looking until it is mounted, and it is unlike English water-colour paper which is stiffish and can stand alone. The surface of rice paper is quite different from that of any other paper. It gives a transient effect that is not easy to define, and I adore it. Occasionally I try my hand on Watman paper, using sable brushes; but my spirit then droops lower and lower instead of soaring. Such is the idiosyncrasy of this humble artist. Watman water-colour paper has a most elegant texture, and if you are careful you can sponge off anything you dislike. Not so with rice paper. Once you have made a mark with your brush, it is there for good and nothing will remove it. Therefore, in painting the rose, I was unable to cover the many mistakes I made, and each time I had to begin all over again, until my brain felt as though it would explode.

When the roses are reproduced, will they be merely eye-catching and meaningless to the buyer; or will some folk, maybe, look further, and see the roses quietly tinged by an ephemeral spirit?

CHAPTER 12

AFTER so many rose paintings, and myself toiling with the well nigh unattainable, I spent my next working hours mostly painting landscapes. They gave me a wider vista of approach, and the world on my rice paper invariably led me to Iceland. As long as there were mountains and water, shrubs and moors – not forgetting waterfalls – I was happy. That is, apart from the painting mistakes that were forever cropping up. Trees in Iceland are scarce, and when my brush is impelled to paint one or more in a landscape, I could almost swear that in the far distance, and without delving into my folio, mountains scallop the horizon. I suppose it is a gentle form of mania!

And in this hankering I am returning to Iceland again.

It is five years since I flew there, and as soon as possible Halldór drove us to Thingvellir. I had stayed there on my two previous visits, and after we made arrangements I stayed again for several days. Thingvellir is Iceland's most sacred place, and to me it is the most enchanting spot I have ever seen. Historically important, too, because in the year 930 the *Althing* (the oldest parliament north of the Alps) assembled at Thingvellir. Motoring slowly down the steep pass one is hemmed on one side by the Almannagjá – a rambling and gigantic lava wall; and on the opposite side, large rocky formations jut through emerald green grass. At the bottom of the pass those rocky hillocks end, and a scene of unforgettable beauty unfolds itself, rather like the transformation of a fairy story. The valley seems to stretch indefinitely, and the deep-rifted plains are bordered by majestic mountains and glaciers. There, too, lies part of Thingvalla Lake, covering an area of nearly seventy square miles. It is island-dappled, and in the summer trout may be caught.

In such a landscape there stands a charming and diminutive church and its vicarage.

Valholl is the only existing hotel for miles around, but one sees summer houses sprinkled about the edge of the lake. Valholl is singularly primitive and has changed only in size since my first visit there before the war.

One captivating morning I was eating breakfast by a window, when I happened to peer through it. Standing outside I noticed a casually dressed and bearded gentleman. Immediately I thought he must be an artist, and as he walked away I wondered who he was. After breakfast I strolled over a bridge and across to the other side of a finger of the lake to look closer at the tiny church. It seemed so innocent and childlike, and absolutely Arcadian. The church was painted white with green shutters and a red roof. Oh, how adorable it was! A minute spire had been picoted in blue, and that completed the picture. Two huge chunks of lava provided steps, and I turned an enormous key and entered the church. Several small pews ran on either side of the aisle, and an oak pulpit was ornamented by white-edged panels and snowy-centred flowers. A big picture of Christ healing the sick looked down upon the Holy Table. This was covered by a red velvet cloth, and on it there stood a golden cross. And in that alluring wafer of space I sat down in silent prayer. How peaceful — how far away it all seemed; yet forever His gentle presence pervaded.

As I left the church and was passing the vicarage next door, I saw the bearded gentleman hauling hay from the front door on to a motor wagon. We smiled and I stopped and spoke to him. In excellent English he told me that he was the Vicar of Thingvellir, and of another diminutive church across the valley. He was also the Keeper of the National Park, and all foreign heads of states visit this idyllic region. As we talked I learned that he had studied in London. Moreover, he spoke fluent Chinese, having spent many years as a missionary in China. Here was yet another strange coincidence, for next morning when I was invited to have coffee with the Vicar and his wife, I noticed that the vicarage was filled with oriental treasures. Everywhere those Chinese masters had left their delicate imprints, for scrolls hung on the walls, and our coffee cups were placed on an embroidered Chinese cloth. But our delicious home-baked edibles were entirely Icelandic!

We had a good talk about the Icelandic church, and about my own church in London, which the Vicar remembered from when he was a student. Unlike the Cathedral in Reykjavik this little church is never closed, but services are usually held in the afternoon. Country folk prefer it, for many of them have to face long rough treks on foot from their solitary farms. Other people travel by pony-back or by car.

I was then able to walk much better than now, and I did not need my stick which, at present, often helps my precarious legs not to fall over when my hare-brain is tired, or not concentrating on where I am going. It is a "dandy" stick, and rather fun to use, and it belonged to my aunt who had no use for it.

At Thingvellir I used to wander around, just staring, and I was so often reminded of those two famous lines from W. H. Davies's poem:

> *What is this life if, full of care,*
> *We have no time to stand and stare?*

I never found it hard to "stand and stare" in that blessed locality, and I know that others felt the same as myself. Before I returned to Gljúfrasteinn, to Halldór and Audur, I bade farewell to the kind Vicar and his wife. They told me that from September until spring Valhöll is closed, as well as a dozen or so private summer houses, and they and their family remain in that panoramic scene, completely alone.

Some months later when I was talking with my Rector about Thingvellir, he agreed with an idea I had for a little article for the church magazine. It was called "An Icelandic

Parson". By degrees I wrote the article and it was published.

How odd it is that some ribbons cling to the mind. For instance, that white wooden cross over the garden gate of the vicarage at Thingvellir still shines for me in the sunlight, as it shone on my last day there . . . or was I dreaming?

On my homeward voyage of discovery with my tempestuous craft rather battered, and myself, the voyager, a little wiser and a lot happier, the inner voice that urged me to continue the tale when I felt like abandoning ship, also urged me, when I was uncertain, to cast doubts to the winds, and to stretch out my hand to Jesus. His is a strong hand and mine so weak. And in doing this the compensations I have found have been prodigious, especially when I have listened to His consoling words. Here are some of them . . .

"To Him the porter openeth; and the sheep hear His voice; and He calleth His own sheep by name, and He leadeth them out.

"And when He putteth forth His own sheep, He goeth before them, and the sheep follow Him: for they know His voice."

As I look back I see, in my mind's eye, a humble white wooden cross over a gate at Thingvellir. I see as well five crosses of various nationalities and sizes, and made of different material: of wood, metal, pearls and palm. They have been given to me by friends. Each cross tells a story, both of the giver, and of the imperceptible thread that links us together; and the cross at Thingvellir not only reminds me of those halcyon days, it reminds me of the words of Jesus when he said: "Deny thyself, take up thy cross and follow me."

During my voyage an actor friend has gone to Heaven. He once gave me a tiny golden cross, and another friend sent me a slender gold chain which is prettily twisted around my wrist, and on which hangs my cross. In sunshine and in shadow it is always there, intermingled with gossamer memories. And my dismantled brain is gradually awakening as though it has been hovering at the chink of a half-open door.

Now the long journey has ended and my ship is safely anchored in harbour. Ebbing green-blue waves have strangely turned dove-grey and a million flickering stars shine. Jesus said "Lo, I am with you alway, even unto the end of the world."

And I believe Him.

PART TWO
1968

CHAPTER 13

I FINISHED the first part of this book over two and a half years ago, but so many things have happened since then that I decided to add the other half to it.

For a time I put the original manuscript aside. I neither felt like writing any more or even trying to paint. Other things took my attention, and they had to be attended to. I became like a sheep on a mountain side, and just grazed and looked around. After a while I decided that I would begin to paint again, but as I ruminated and doodled my mind did not stumble on a suitable subject to paint. I wanted to change my ideas but nothing came my way to re-charge them. All I knew was that I longed to paint, but I was waiting to kindle my imagination through a different channel of thought.

Perhaps my thoughts were wandering too far ahead, and the nervous tendrils of my brain snapped a little, because I slipped on some damp leaves and broke my right hand! As I was alone and near my studio I reached there somehow, and I opened the door and sat down. The shock and pain were quite shattering. It happened to be on a Sunday night, yet it never occurred to me to telephone for an ambulance to take me to a hospital where a casualty department would be open. Early the next morning I went to my own hospital. The hand was X-rayed. Yes, I was told, the hand was broken and would have to be plastered nearly to the elbow. Chores were awkward to cope with, and friends often came along and cooked meals that would last for a day or two.

Gradually I learned to do things with my left hand, including writing. That was not easy, but I enjoyed trying to master it, and some people told me that my left hand writing was much better than my normal right hand script! The letters were larger and more decipherable, and really quite different from the usual hasty notes. It was fun because many single letters seemed to turn into the most extra-ordinary shapes. Anything I wanted to write took me ages to do. Often I thought that it might be a jolly good thing for everyone to write with the other hand (left or right), then if something happened to the injured one, the good hand would prove its worth. After a long time the plaster was removed, and although the right hand was weak from being in plaster, I exercised it, and gradually it got better.

Not long after this—in fact one morning in March, 1965—I heard the postman push some letters through my letter box. On picking them up I glanced quickly through them. The large handwriting I knew so well fascinated me, so I opened that envelope first. I read the letter several times. Was I dreaming or was I really taking in what the letter said? For, to my utter surprise, the friend whose letter I had just read told me that an anonymous donor had heard my broadcasts, and was very interested in my well being, and also of my love of Iceland. Would I like to go again and visit my Icelandic friends and to stay for a month as before? The donor was to remain absolutely anonymous and would never disclose the identity although my friend knew who it was.

I asked only two questions: Did I know the person?

"No," said my friend.

And would I rob him or her of any money if I went?

"No," again answered my friend. "You can be quite happy about everything." She was so hoping I would say yes, and although my heart was anything but at ease, I was breath-less with excitement at the thought of it. Jesus had indeed solved my problems for me and in a most unexpected way.

"Yes, yes," I cried thankfully. "It's simply wonderful."

First of all I had to write to my Icelandic friends. For all I knew they might have arranged to go away for some months, which is often their custom. Then there were clothes and shoes and so on. The anonymous donor had kindly provided me with a certain amount of money for such necessities, Halldór and Audur answered my letter immediately by telegram. It said that all would be well if

I went on a certain day in June. Gradually all was settled, and the kind friend who had arranged everything for me, drove me to the airport. Once more I found myself sitting in the Viking plane and flying again to Iceland. How unbelievably good God is.

When I was in hospital with a second cerebral haemorrhage, my Rector gave me a little paper book called *Words of Comfort*. He knew that it was not easy for me to read, and in this book the print is large and good. I read a page each day and then I begin again. I had put this little book in my handbag, so I took it out and turned to the last page – the thirty-first day. The last line ran: "I will trust and not be afraid." Then I put the book back in my bag and tried hard not to be afraid. As I looked down through the window of the plane, and for hours saw nothing but the sea, my heart beat violently at times. I watched the whirling mass of water below, turbulent in some areas, while at other times all seemed to be calm, interweaving and shining like a great aquamarine jewel. When we were having a delicious meal I asked my neighbour whether she preferred my seat next to the window or her inside seat. She said she would like mine best, so we exchanged seats, and we both felt happier. My consultant had suggested that earlier, when we were talking about the trip, for height can do odd things for me and my brain.

Actually the flight was smooth, and I am so grateful to have now tasted flying many times. This time, even from my inside seat in the plane, I could just recognise those familiar outlines jutting out of the sea. Then the spots became larger and those glorious glaciers loomed like magic in the evening sunlight. Soon we had flown past them, and bits of buildings caught my heart: I knew where we were. Slowly the plane descended and the Viking eventually halted on the tarmac of the small airport of Reykjavik.

Here everything was much the same, and for a wonder it was not raining! In the middle of trying to find one another I saw Audur rushing into the booking office. She had been held up, but now she was there, and that was all that mattered. Halldór had also been kept, and could not come until some hours later. We gabbled excitedly in happiness, and then jumped into Audur's car. "Did I feel equal to going to the new flat first?" she enquired. She would so like to show it to me. By now it was about nine thirty, and actually I felt rather exhausted. But everything was so thrilling, and of course it was almost daylight by Icelandic standards, so we quickly drove to the flat, not too far away.

"Please, Jesus," I said to myself, "please will you give me strength?" And He did.

As we drove nearer Reykjavik I saw that many buildings had been erected, both flats and houses. There seemed to be no particular plans, and it was just as haphazard looking as I always remember. Frequently Audur turned into a side street. It was unmade as so many other streets are, but you soon get accustomed to that in Iceland. On one side of the street the buildings were old and timbered and coloured, while on the other side there was a new block of flats. On the first floor I had my first glimpse of my friends' flat. It had a Scandinavian interior with its beautiful wooden walls and so forth, and the furniture and curtains either came from Sweden, Denmark or Finland. Like Gljúfrasteinn the bathroom was delightful in tiles of white and blue, with a blue bath. The big windows of the large room contained a Bechstein grand piano, Halldór's desk and bookshelves and other odds and ends. Near the wall opposite stood a refectory table and chairs. A small dining partition with a little balcony overlooked the same view of sea and mountains. I had often wondered about the flat with so much nostalgia, and here I was! A little *cri de coeur* issued from me. As far as I could see there were no disappointments, and Audur told me that I could stay in the flat whenever I wished to be alone.

Eventually we drove home, fifteen miles away, on the now familiar curving road among the mountains and hot springs, interspersed by a few farms and cattle. Even as we talked I saw in the distance, and standing on a hillock Gljúfrasteinn, the home I never expected to see again. As we stood in the hall I cast my glance around. Everything looked much the same. Maybe a picture had been changed for another. Fair-haired Sigga, now fourteen, ran down the stairs to meet me, and dark-haired Duna, who, seven years ago, had been four now danced from the garden. The girls were quite unsophisticated and they plastered their bedrooms with Beatle photographs. They enjoy pony riding over the moors better than anything else, and although they travel a great deal with their parents, they are never so happy as when they return home again. There they are carefree in the simple life they love. It was a happy family, and when Halldór tore in breathless from his appointment the family seemed complete. What a tremendous lot there was to say.

By twelve o'clock we staggered to bed – I in a different bedroom this time. From the window the view was covered in splendour, and as I gazed with awe at the long range of mountains before me I was quite unashamed of my tears, for I had never ceased to wonder at their grave majesty. The sight of mountains everywhere had never frightened me. Their quality of inevitability gave me strength.

This visit was to be a real holiday, and I was told to do nothing, except to rest. That meant doing no writing or painting, and indeed no parties, since Icelanders love parties. It was difficult to go to bed early, say about nine, which is my usual time at home, because the nights were never dark. I usually did my letter writing and cards in bed about midnight, or in the early morning when everything was quiet. Furthermore, however late they go to bed, Icelanders rise early. Our breakfast time was eight and if the girls insisted on sitting up late they were made to arise for breakfast just the same.

Objects in the dining-room were much as before. It was all so simple and uncluttered. Yet one thing had changed. Along one wide wall there used to be a needlework tapestry depicting some part of Icelandic life. When I first went to Iceland I noticed that most households had one hanging on the walls. It was a traditional custom, and Audur's mother had made this big needlework tapestry. Now it had been transferred to a wall of the long music room. In its place hung a large oil painting. At meal times I used to look at it as it faced me where I sat. It was so unusual, and the painting seemed to have a strange aura about it. At last I enquired about its being. Halldór told me the long history, and how he brought it home in the back of his car, after a tiring day. The picture was a large vertical oil, and was not easy to place. So, after days of wondering they decided to re-hang the needlework tapestry near the Steinway, and put the painting in its place in the dining-room. And there I saw it on my last visit in 1965.

Gradually the painting haunted me, for I looked at it frequently, in fact each time I walked into the dining-room, which was often. It was of "The Baptism of Christ in Iceland". The painting was an early one by Kjarval, now over eighty years old, and considered to be Iceland's most celebrated painter. Originally the picture was considered for the altar of a small church in North Iceland—but that is another story. Halldór remembered the painting when he first saw it many years ago. Later it was stored in an attic, and later still it hung in a farmhouse. In between times many other things had happened. Halldór heard of its whereabouts and called to see the owner of the painting who, he had heard, was hard up. She was delighted to sell the painting when she saw the nice fat cheque he offered her, and he was just as thrilled to become the owner of such a beautiful and poignant picture. It had been badly damaged and torn, but when I saw it a restorer had carefully mended is as best he could.

In the painting, Jesus as a boy kneels in supplication. His hands are clasped as He looks up at John the Baptist. A dove hovers about Jesus as His halo of pale yellow star points outlines His boyish head. The Christ Child wears a short tunic over His narrow trousers, which are the colour of dark salmon. John the Baptist's robes are more sombre but of the same hue, and each is barefooted. The colours are so harmonious although they are not what most of us imagine them to be. But why should not Christ be baptised in Iceland? The artist used his own imagination and without doubt he was doubly inspired in this painting. He chose for his background the enormous lava formation known as Almannagjá, and a lovely blue trickle of the waterfall called Oxarafoss runs down the lava and around the Baptist's right hand, thereby baptising Jesus as he lays his hand on the youthful head. In the distance there is a tiny part of the wonderful lake of Thingvellir as well as mountains behind it. A few Icelandic wild flowers grow near the feet of Jesus.

A few days before I left Iceland I had a sudden urge to write down what I saw in front of me, just in case I might forget. The story was really quite long, but these lines are just the bare silhouette.

The studio welcomed me as ever on my return, for I always love the sight of it as I turn my key in the lock. It took me some time to get accustomed to my own way of living, and also to my "early to bed" nights. I do not remember painting much when I settled down. Writing always had been what I longed to do, but as ideas were so difficult to think out, no editor gave me a chance to prove my worth. Also my days now were quite different from the time when I was a busy journalist and I was obliged to finish articles by a certain day or date.

Yet I have never really given up. I read as much as I can, even though I remember little, and I do try to persevere. If I am especially interested in the book I am reading, then I plod through the pages heedless of the many sentences I leave out. And I read the Bible quite a lot—in my own way.

One thing I especially remember in Iceland is that haunting painting of Christ being baptised in Iceland. One morning I looked at the notes I made there regarding the picture, and I decided to write a little article, merely for my own pleasure. Later I went to see my Rector, and as I was telling him about the painting I passed him the short typewritten article I had written, never thinking he would be particularly interested. To my utter surprise he asked me whether I would lend the article to him, and I said of course he could do what he liked with it. Then I thought no more about it. Many weeks later there came a cheque from *The Church of England Newspaper*. It was for my little article which I had completely forgotten. My Rector had shown it to the editor who apparently liked it and published it. As it was nearing Christmas the paper with my article in it and the cheque had been mislaid. So when they arrived so unexpectedly it was a delightful surprise. Especially as I was in hospital again.

CHAPTER 14

ABOUT three weeks before Christmas 1965, I went to see
my consultant in the hospital. The previous evening I had
felt extremely dizzy . . . much more so than usual. The
following morning the dizziness was no better, and when
I was pulling back the curtains I had to cling to a chair in
order to save myself from falling down. The same thing
happened when I was making the bed, but in that instance
I fell over the bed and so I was saved from the floor! When
I telephoned my kind neighbour and friend to tell her of
my predicament, she at once said she would drive me to the
hospital, as fortunately she was driving that way. She also
said she would pick me up on her way back. She left me at
the hospital and we went on our separate errands. I was still
terribly dizzy and could not understand it.

My consultant, who took my blood pressure after hearing
my tale, was horrified – or so it seemed. He looked at me
and then he said, "I want you in hospital right away. Your
blood pressure has suddenly soared."

"Now?" I asked him.

"Yes," he replied, "*now*. Unless you want to have a third
stroke." I was shocked and I could scarcely believe it.

"But," I said, "I have all my Christmas presents to pack
and send."

"Well," he said, "I shall not be responsible for the
possible consequences if you don't stay here."

We talked as I lay on the bed and I tried to recover from
the shock. I said I would do what he asked me to do, but
would he allow me to return home and fetch some night
clothes and toilet things? Obviously there was no time
regarding Christmas presents. They would just have to stay
where they were.

As my friend would be waiting outside the hospital with
her car, my kind consultant agreed to allow me to go home

and collect my things—that is, he said, if my friend would drive me back to the hospital by three o'clock. This she kindly agreed to do, and when we arrived back at the studio I did things slowly, trying to have no thought for the presents I had so carefully laid out, and which meant so much to me. I put the Christmas cards in my case so that I might address them in bed, together with my Bible and a book of poems. Then my friends drove me back to the hospital in good time, and left me there. By now I was fairly used to this sort of thing but not always at Christmas time! A few hours later my consultant came to see me in the ward. I was so glad to see him, for he calmed my ruffled nerves. He promised me that if all went well he would allow me to leave a day or two before Christmas so that I might go home. That cheered me no end because I was expecting to spend Christmas Day with a friend. Alas, it was not to be.

For the first week the high blood pressure would not decrease, although it was taken frequently. I was kept in bed for the first week and not allowed to get up. The ward seemed so terribly hot to me although no one else thought the same. I was not given any tablets that week, and in any case I loathed them. Then the treatment began in the hopes that the high blood pressure would decrease. Firstly I was given pills to try out the dosage. The pills seemed very strong and I felt I wanted to sleep most of the time. I was so glad to see my friends in the evening, and when it was time for the blood pressure to be taken they were asked to remain outside the cubicle until it was finished.

Breakfasts are extremely early in hospitals, and I asked whether I might have a bath before breakfast. I was given permission and walked to the bathroom, feeling dizzy and unsteady. Still it seemed so blissful to me to be going to have a bath, and I meant to get into it at all costs—which I did! Then I looked down at myself. To my horror I saw that my body and legs and arms were covered with red spots! Even my face and my scalp irritated me. I called to a nurse and she came into the bathroom. I pointed to the spots. By that time I thought I must have scarlet fever. She told me to dry myself and return to bed as quickly as possible. Sister came to look at me, and then a house physician arrived, and after a good examination of my spots, they were found to be caused by the tablets I was given. So they were changed and fresh pills prescribed, and in three days the spots disappeared, for which I was very thankful.

Lovely Christmas cards were sent to me in hospital, and my locker was covered with them. Some Christmas presents also arrived, but within myself I thought of what my consultant had told me earlier. "I'll let you go home before Christmas if I think you are fit enough to go," he had said. The pills had rather drained me. One morning I had more or less fainted before breakfast, and I felt terribly weak. So again I was not allowed to get up that day. I was quite happy to stay in bed and to close my eyes. I did not feel like talking or even listening. Most people, I think, who have brain trouble of one sort or another, enjoy being quiet and saying little, and if it is at all possible to sleep in a private ward or in an amenity ward, or with another patient with similar trouble. I am perfectly sure that this is the best way to help a sensitive sufferer. Of course things are not always possible, but there should be much more publicity regarding cerebral haemorrhages. We hear about most illnesses but this one we seldom do. It is kept in the dark, probably because it is incurable and can go on indefinitely, with the patient fermenting inwardly and with no one to try to help, apart from feeding them and so on.

To me these are some of the saddest illnesses there are, mainly because the brain has been affected. I would so love to help people who suffer in this way. It has always been an uphill battle in my case, and I know it always will be. But if you, like myself, believe in Jesus wholly, and you give your heart to Him to keep, He will help you if you ask Him; even if you are unable to utter a word. Remember, Jesus Christ said: "I will not leave you comfortless: I will come to you."

Patients who suffer from one or more cerebral haemorrhages need endless patience. They find it difficult to grasp the simplest situation. A friend or teacher who understands these problems has to repeat the same word over and over again in order to try to make the patient understand its meaning. I remember when I first broadcast a talk about how I managed to eventually speak and read, a listener with a brother who suffered from the same complaint as mine wrote to me and asked various questions. He came to tea, and between us we suggested several things. The brother was in hospital again, and when I saw him he was looking wonderfully well, yet for the last year he had been quite unable to speak at all. And like myself he could understand all that was said to him. The consultant and the ward sister were extremely kind and allowed me to suggest what I thought best for him. So I decided to go every afternoon to the hospital, and armed with a few empty exercise books I sat by his bedside and began.

I had never taught anyone in my life, and this was a real beginning. He was a big, jolly man with a smiling face, and at first he did not seem to want to do anything, but I talked to him, and gradually he listened. I wrote his Christian name in large printed letters in one of the exercise books. Then I pointed to each letter, and presently he was able to say his name – or bits of it, even though no one else might understand. By the following day he had forgotten it. However, I expected that. I also made little drawings on each page such as a bird, a mouse, a flower and so on, and underneath it I printed what the drawing was called. By degrees he would try very hard to say the word of the drawing I had made. Naturally each word was as simple as the drawing. If the patient did not feel like doing anything I would not press him. He appeared extremely happy in the ward, and the other patients who knew that he could not speak never left him out of their conversations. One afternoon when I went to see him the ward sister told me that he would have to have a small operation – nothing to do with the cerebral haemorrhage. The operation should have been done more than a year ago, but he would not agree. At that time he was well in health. The physical trouble had flared up again and there was no choice.

The operation was performed and he recovered within a week. But the idea of trying to speak again did not appeal to him, and no one wanted to force him. I often went to see him in his private ward, and presently he was moved to a delightful nursing home. I went there once with a relative of his, but we did not think that he really remembered me, so I did not go again. I have often thought of him and have wondered what happened to him. He had a private nurse always, and in his case his relatives were all much attached to him, so I knew he would be well looked after. He was not an old man, though many years older than myself; those who are really old seldom have the strength to battle with this illness.

A cerebral haemorrhage is a fairly common complaint, but it is rarely talked about simply because the patients infrequently recover their normal activities such as speaking, writing and reading. Even then, after a short while the patient becomes tired and finds it difficult to think clearly, especially when the subject needs much thought. The same applies to writing and reading. Although it is two or three years ago since I wrote the first half of this little book, it is almost just as difficult to write what I am trying hard to think out, and to read what I have written. My pages are covered with crossings out, and with trying to get my sentences correct. So I do hope my readers will forgive my bad English. An artist friend has kindly helped me to improve them.

My small ship is sailing forth again, out of the harbour and into the wide open sea. And the sea is often troublesome. It is laden with irrepressibly formidable waves that are not easy to steer through. Yet, so far, we have survived with the help of God. "The Lord's hand is not shortened, that it cannot save; neither his ear heavy, that it cannot hear." I often wonder how He can hear the slightest piteous tapping on His ear. Yet He does hear—always.

Returning to my stay in hospital over two years ago, I was having an afternoon siesta when two unknown doctors came to see me. They said they would like to have a thorough examination of my right eye, and would I mind? They were especially kind and thoughtful, so why should I mind? They spent about two hours looking into my right eye, and I imagine by then that they were just as tired as I was. They thanked me and left. The next day they appeared again and did the same thing. Apparently they saw something behind the eye, although so far nothing had appeared. The day my consultant told me I might go home (two days before Christmas) a radiographer arrived. She particularly wished to photograph the right eye. First of all though, and every ten minutes or so, a nurse was told to squeeze a number of drops into the eye. In the meantime I had to lie quite still. This went on for about an hour, and by that time I could not see at all through the bad eye. The radiographer came to fetch me, and she led me down the stairs to the X-ray room. There she took a number of photographs of the right eye in different positions. When the position was quite correct a blinding light was switched on and the X-ray was taken. It took ages to get everything right, and I must say that whole operation was extremely tiring, although I was sitting down on a kind of form looking into this large X-ray machine. When it was all finished the radiographer led me back to the ward and she asked me to lie on my bed until the effects had subsided. So instead of returning home in the morning as I had expected, I was not able to go until the afternoon. My kind neighbour had telephoned to say that she was calling for me in her car.

On my return home the first things I saw in the studio were the presents on the big table ready to be posted for Christmas. Everything had seemed like a dream, and still was to me. I was very dizzy, and I had been given some strong pills to bring home. I had also to promise that I would take them, five a day, and at certain times. It did not seem a bit like Christmas, and all I longed for was to lie down and to waft away with Jesus' warm cadences around me: "I, even I, am he that comforteth you." Yes, I thought, Jesus would always comfort me. I telephoned my friend who lived miles away, and told her that I must be alone on Christmas Day, and that, after all, I could not possibly join her. She offered to fetch me in her car if only I would go, but alas, I knew it was hopeless, and I did not want to spoil the Christmas festivities which I knew would be going on. How perfect it was just to be alone after nearly three weeks of constant activities! My brain had been feverishly counting the days till my return home, and by now I was quite indifferent of solitude. I loved it. And I loved listening to the small boys in the street outside who seemed to have no idea how to keep in tune, nor indeed of the meaning of the lovely carols. So long as they were given sixpence they were content. As I lay in bed on Christmas Eve I remembered that I went to sleep with the strains of "Once in royal David's city".

Today was Christmas Day, and for the first time in my life I was spending it alone. I had often wondered what it would be like, and now I knew. It was my own wish, for I did not feel equal to doing anything—only to sit quietly by the fire, take the various pills, think of the Holy Babe, and try to sweep away the sad thoughts from my mind.

During the afternoon, and most unexpectedly, a loud knock sounded on my door. I opened it, and there stood the friend who knows that anonymous donor, and who had been the means of my flying back to Iceland. She had just driven over, she said, for a short while, and had left her party to get on with the washing-up in her absence! I was delighted to see her, and as she had visited me in hospital she knew that I could not talk for long. She had brought me some of her home-made mince-pies as well as a big slice of her iced Christmas cake. It was such a wonderful thought of hers, almost like a ray of sunshine gliding into the studio. I shall never forget it. Soon afterwards she left to return to her party, while I sat down once more gazing into the firelight and plunging back into my own thoughts.

At the end of the following week I was asked to return to

the hospital. I was extremely dizzy, and my friend next door drove me there. One of the same house physicians examined me and then gave me still another tablet, thinking that they might bring my high blood pressure down still further. In the first place I had never been fond of pills, as my consultant knew, and I took them only when he asked me to – which was not often. However, when I next went to see him he reduced the pills by one or two. There were usually so many things to talk over, and the New Year 1966 had begun.

CHAPTER 15

In March a most unpleasant event happened. I met a friend who had kindly offered to help me buy curtain materials in a special shop in the West End. She seemed worried about me and kept insisting that I sat down for a few minutes. The materials were so ravishing that it was difficult to choose the right patterns. We had been there for over two hours before we had some tea, and although it had all been so engrossing we were glad to go home. I was still taking two or three of the large and nasty pills although they had not decreased my dizziness.

The following afternoon I decided to have an afternoon bath, as a friend was coming to an early supper. This I did and very fortunately I had towelled myself and was standing on the bath rug. After that I remembered nothing more until I opened my eyes and found myself lying full length on the rug! I must have fainted without knowing that it was going to happen. I expected to jump up quickly and get dressed, but when I tried to do so I found myself unable to move as my back was paralysed. So I lay there wondering what to do. I had closed all the windows, and I could not shout or scream for no one would hear me. Then I tried to lift up my arms. They were not paralysed, but they were so weak that they flopped back beside me. I tried to roll around on my side, but it was of no avail. I was helpless. For some time I lay there, with my eyes closed. Surely God would come to my rescue. He always had done so before. Presently I tried again. My arms were desperately weak, but this time I managed to cling to the edge of the bath. Alas, nothing came of it because once more my arms flopped – and so did I. Still, my back was not now quite as paralysed. A little later I tried again, and this time I managed to roll over slightly – but I soon rolled back! There was no strength left. And so it went on.

Eventually, after what I felt was a Herculean roll, I managed by degrees to get on to my knees. Then I clung desperately to the edge of the bath, fearing that I would let go at any minute. From the bath to the basin was only a matter of several inches, although it seemed to me like yards. But I made it. I somehow struggled on to my feet, and my back, although weak, had loosened itself. I felt so shaky and queer that I hardly dared move. If only I could manoeuvre a way to reach my dressing gown . . . And I did – somehow. Then I sat on a cedar box that was near me and wondered what to do. If only – oh, if only I could get to my telephone at the other end of the studio, but that was of no use – I couldn't.

Next I clung to odd pieces of furniture and tried to walk to a chair. By inches I reached a chair, only a few yards away, and sat down trembling and hazy, but all in a piece. Then I glanced at the telephone on my bookcase and wondered whether I would ever be able to reach it. And I thought of Jesus who said, "Fear thou not for I am with thee." Of course He would help me to stagger to the telephone. He would never leave me in the lurch. So I made a gambling effort to stand up and walk to the telephone somehow. And I did manage it, shaking and almost incoherent. A stool was always there, and gratefully I sat down on it. By then my strength had emerged a little and I looked for the number I needed. My consultant was not there but he would be given my message and would telephone me on his return. After that I gradually moved to a chair nearby and sat by the fire.

Now if only I could make a cup of tea, I thought, I would feel much better. At the moment I had not the strength to open a window, and my friend was out at present. The only thing I could do would be to make another attempt to reach the kitchen. Little by little, and clinging on to anything, I found the kitchen. The tray was already laid and the kettle soon boiled. But to take it to the fire and sit there was a formidable task! However I managed it, and without breaking anything! Then I sat down shaking and quivering. My back had almost unlocked itself but I was afraid to move.

Unexpectedly someone knocked on my door. I spoke as loudly as I could, asking whoever was there to please wait until I was able to open the door. Never had I been more thankful to see a stranger, for I had seen her only once or twice before. After she had left a friend called. By then I somehow felt that the worst was over, and that she need not worry about leaving me alone. So she went home and I went to bed. It had been a kind of nightmare, and as I was so tired with all that had happened I fell sound asleep. Being alone seldom worries me. I know that God will look after me if I ask Him.

The following morning my consultant telephoned me, and after a talk he asked me to go and see him at the hospital in a few days time if I felt able to go. The friend next door, in her goodness, drove me there, and then went her way. I was so glad to see my consultant and to have a talk with him. He always encourages me instead of discouraging me from my activities and my madcap career – such as it is now – and I seldom ask him the cause of these unpleasant happenings. He listens with kindly attention to my outpourings, whatever they are, and makes notes of them. On the whole I say little about this illness but I know he understands. I much prefer to tell him about what I am trying to write, or to paint. If I am unable to get on with these things – the things I love and have struggled for, then he knows, without any explanation, that something is wrong. Naturally I conceal some truths to myself, particularly the grief that lies too deep for words. For this grief has thwarted me for over twelve years. Yet I thank God for helping me gradually to emerge from that dark abyss and into the light where words beat like singing voices in my ear, and I am able miraculously to turn the pages without closing the book at the end of one short sentence.

Oh, how I long to help others with cerebral haemorrhages, especially those who have no desire to battle any longer. I can tell them that the battle is worth while fighting for, even though there is nothing outwardly to show for it, and few people realise the solitary isolation it entails.

My consultant was making notes as I talked. Then I said:
"If you don't mind I would rather not take any more tablets."

He looked at me gently and then he said: "Will you take
three tablets a day?"

"No," I answered "not even ONE."

He had known me for a long time and knew my determined ideal. So he continued writing and said nothing.

Then I murmured something about, "If you would really
like me to take one tablet daily, I'll do that." But again he
said nothing.

I had always tried to do what he asked me to do, but this
time the very thought of taking those pills seemed to throttle
me. As I left him he said: "Come again next week, and we'll
see how you are without them."

I stood up and felt pretty queer.

"How are you getting home?" he enquired.

"Oh, I don't know," I said, inwardly feeling like a som-
nambulist besmirched with dizziness, and I knew that I
could not possibly cross a road without being run over.

"Sit down in Out Patients," he continued as he looked
straight at me, "and I'll arrange for an ambulance to take
you back."

I thanked him and gratefully sat down there for a short
while. Presently a nurse called me and took me to the
ambulance and I was driven home. In my experience ambulance men are always extremely kind and gentle, and they
have a great sense of humour, which indeed they need. After
the studio door was opened for me they left, and I reflected
on what had happened that morning.

This particular dizziness continued for many weeks. In
bed it was just the same. I couldn't turn over without feeling
as though I was falling out of bed, or that the bed was floating beneath me. But I had known this dizziness, and far
worse, when I was attacked by a second cerebral haemorrhage. Then I dared not move at all. My brain had no con-
trol whatsoever. Eventually I ventured to do a little shopping in the neighbourhood, and I tried to preserve the
appearance of normality. That was not easy, nor indeed has

it ever been: but imagination is not usually the lot of most humans especially in this age and time. The world is a materialistic and money-spinning orb with too little respect for the gentler things of life. Some day, no doubt, all will change again, when everything is not bogged down with generalisations. Creative impulses will surely once more stir up romantic visions of the rose-bush path and the canopied trees; and the lovely clouds invading the hills. Those mysterious perfections have an unearthly beauty that is beyond all comprehension. They are the "pearls of great price". Let us not forget them.

The things I enjoy most are the gaily expressed symbols of colour everywhere. The streets, the gay umbrellas and the shop windows—what fun it is to gaze at them! Colour should make us feel happy and give us pleasure which surely assuages our many fatigues, although for me I cannot always sniff the rose-scented air, nor see the silver light breaking through the clouds.

By degrees the intense dizziness grew a little less, and I began to feel much better. One morning, just before I left to see my consultant in hospital, a letter arrived that completely took my breath away. I will not disclose what it was because the thought of it is as disquieting as the whips of pain that sometimes attack my thinking. Such a shock as this had never entered my head, and a dreadful lucidity made the letter all the clearer. I was afraid of losing my mind, and once more I was standing on the brink of an abyss. As I was putting on my coat I asked God to protect me. Then I picked up the little paper-covered book my Rector gave me when I was in hospital. I opened it and saw "Trust ye in the Lord forever". Of course God would not desert me, nor indeed would my true friends.

It was difficult to surmount the contents of the letter I held. Yet I must leave it to God. For a moment a fearful sense of solitude surrounded me. Then as suddenly as it had appeared it vanished, and those unshed tears that had almost choked me were lost in the void. I opened the door, and pulling it behind me, walked slowly towards the hospital. God had divined my thoughts and He allowed me to go on with my dreaming. My thoughts usually take hold of me and I am unable to catch them and put them in some sort of order. Actually I was thinking about my last holiday in Iceland.

CHAPTER 16

THE weather, which is always a major part of a holiday, was reasonably good although at times it could have been warmer. The large grounds of Gljúfrasteinn had been groomed a great deal since my last visit, and a swimming pool had been added. It was really quite fantastic. The pool was heated from hot springs, and it had blue and white tiles to decorate it. At the bottom of the garden's wild parts the stream gurgled as ever before, and you could sit on the huge boulders if you were near enough to them. Over the moors the small mountains near kept guard over our privacy. Could anything be more idyllic? I had not been able to bathe since I was first ill, much as I had always loved swimming, but it was a delightful distraction to watch others as I sat on the edge of the pool. The silvery stream below had forever given me endless joy, and as I write this sentence the landscape everywhere gives me a thousand memories.

One of my thoughts was Thingvellir. Would Halldór and Audur mind if I stayed there for a few days? Alas, they told me, Valholl had changed hands and the new owner now charged about three times or four times as much as in 1958. Of course we would drive over, and we did—many times. Once we picnicked there, and I hovered about like a ghost who had lost her way, leaving fleeing smiles and wiping cheeks and lips that were wet with tears. Yes, Valholl had changed but only in size. A large shop had been added, and two dining-rooms for the many trippers. The bedrooms and wash basins were much the same as before, so too was the scanty entrance hall. I looked across the small lap of water to the tiny church and its vicarage. They looked exactly the same, but Johann Hannesson and his wife no longer lived there. He had become Professor of Theology at the University of Reykjavik, and they lived on the outskirts. A sad quiet melody touched my heart. Valholl had changed outwardly, but Thingvellir scarcely at all. The large expanse of tideless lake backed by majestic mountains and glaciers was filled with emotion for me. The huge key of the church door had disappeared. It had been locked and I doubted whether I should ever see the inside of it again.

Icelanders are not on the whole a religious race, although from what I have seen they must be among some of the kindest people alive. We were parking the car in Reykjavik when I noticed a man with a beard coming our way. On seeing us he stopped, and to my delight I found that he was none other than Johann Hannesson. He had not forgotten me, nor indeed had I forgotten him. After a long chat he arranged for Audur and myself to have tea with him and his wife in their flat. This we did. In this cheerful flat I remembered many Chinese objects about that were once in the vicarage in Thingvellir. I had again brought him some pamphlets from my own church in London, and we had a delightful talk. The years for me were misted with a mask of gaiety and of sorrow and it was not easy for me to think clearly and to talk easily. Still it had been a lovely afternoon in every way, and as we walked down the many steps from the front door to the pavement I thought of the words of Jesus who said, "My strength is made perfect in weakness." Indeed He had given me the strength all along on this wonderful holiday, and it really had seemed like a gift from Heaven.

I spent a few days on my own in the flat in Reykjavik just browsing around in the neighbourhood, and I loved it. Gudmunder Einarsson, the sculptor, had recently died since I was last there and I missed him. He was a tall, handsome man with his head-hugging astrakhan hat and his waistcoat fastened with silver buttons. I look at the "Mother and Child" pottery group he once gave me with silent recollection and nostalgia.

Many of the streets and shops had been modernised, while others bore their age with dignity. As I crossed the various streets I came to the Cathedral in the centre of Reykjavik. Would the door be opened, I wondered, for in the past it was always locked! I turned the knob, and to my surprise it opened. Then I saw that the church was full of people, so I walked in quietly and sat down at the back. There at the front of the church lay a white coffin. It was obviously a funeral service and much the same as ours although I could not understand the language. I stayed until the end. The bearers carried the white coffin out and I noticed that a bunch of deep red roses lay on top of it. Roses are cherished in Iceland, and those beautiful red roses seemed to pour out their perfume in remembrance. Later I was told that in Iceland coffins are always white and not brown as ours. I did not see another funeral service, although I passed the small Cathedral many times.

In the flat the large window of the sitting-room with its view over the sea had a long bookcase. There were masses of Halldór's books, all in various languages. Those in Icelandic had been bound in leather by an Icelandic publisher, and he had given them to Audur. I enjoyed taking one or two down and glancing through them, although I could not read a word. At other times when I was alone for a few hours in the flat, I would walk down to the sea. It was about ten or fifteen minutes walk away from the flat, over stones and unmade strips of roads. The beach was composed of huge boulders and large rocks, but at low tide the sea ebbed a little, although I never saw any golden sands in that part of Iceland. It was mostly solitary, but occasionally I saw fishermen drying their nets or mending their boats in a certain area. I loved that part of Reykjavik. Not many people wandered along there, but some houses faced the sea, and their gardens ran down to the road. The air was windy though ravishing, and I often stood about contemplating, and looking into memories that had been locked up since my very first visit there. What was the secret of its hold on me?

Although at Gljúfrasteinn I wandered over the moors on the opposite side of the stream, Halldór, unknown to me, followed me with his field glasses from his wide-windowed study. I would slide down a bank and find a grassy mound where I would sit beside the stream, watching its never ending lappings. I always took a notebook and pencil in my bag, although I was content to be idle and to do nothing, except to gather fragments in my heart and to talk with God. Occasionally one or two sheep paid me an unexpected visit as I sat there, deep in thought. They would stand quite still gazing at me with their sad eyes. I never think of looking at sheep without that haunting verse which runs: "I am the Good Shepherd. The Good Shepherd giveth His life for the sheep. My sheep hear My voice and I know them, and they follow Me." After a while I would stumble back and look across to the house, staggering over the bumpy ground that was certainly a little irksome at times and pretty precarious for such as myself. I never minded wandering about on my own—picking a few *fifa* flowers here and there, or a specially beautiful wild flower I had not seen before. I would carry them back with me and put them in water in a jam jar on the writing table in my bedroom. Before I left, Sigga and Duna told me that they would press them for me so that I could take them back to London. I remember seeing them stretched on the floor and pressing the flowers. Now an earthen jug that came from the Holy Land holds my Icelandic *fifa*.

As Audur had her own car, I went with her to many places of call. One whole day we spent driving to see the Great Geysir. Those gaunt and bleak patches of desolate ground were truly fantastic. Small geysirs spouted everywhere, mostly on little hills, and the wet muddy ground underfoot was warmed by them. We walked over it to the Great Geysir, hoping that it would spout soon. It had been erratic for many years and we had to watch it carefully in case it began its boiling spouting. A large round pool housed its centre, and quite soon we heard its rumbling moan. It was time to draw back further and further as the fountain began to play, rearing its deceitfully innocent glories that boiled and lashed the air—but alas, only for a few seconds. Then it gradually died down and we saw no more of it. I picked up numerous bits of what had been boiling water, and I have them beside me now.

The same day we drove to Laugarvatn, a warm lake that is much loved by Icelanders. In parts it is very primitive. As we walked along we opened the door of a hut, and there we saw a great many bathers sitting in their swim suits, having Turkish baths! The heat came from a geysir nearby. The hut was dark inside, and there was no light at all except when someone like ourselves opened the door. I could hardly believe that all the steam inside there was flourishing from a geysir! I must admit that I would not have enjoyed myself in that condensed heat. The landscape in that neighbourhood seemed more human than around the Great Geysir, and numerous houses had been built and were scattered about haphazardly. A large school near the lake opens its doors to visitors in the summer and becomes a hotel. Lots of schools in Iceland do the same, and some are good to stay in. But nowhere and nothing is cheap in that far away land.

We arrived home tired after our long day. Audur had naturally seen everything before, and many times too, but in my case all was new, and as I had no driving problems I just lay back and gazed at the infinities around us. Audur is a splendid driver, so I was never afraid on those treacherous roads although some of them can be quite ruthless. In the distance we had seen Hekla, its snowy-capped mountain top shining in the sunshine. The newly erupted mountain Surtsey lay many miles away, and it would have meant an hour's flight to reach it. My friends had been there, but I was quite happy to stay on dry land and pore into the pregnant silences that lay around me.

My perfect holiday was drawing to its end. I had made very few notes, so I now rely on my thoughts and my dreams. One morning at breakfast Halldór unexpectedly informed us that by a certain time we were to be dressed and ready to go to the National Theatre in Reykjavik. He had taken a box and we were all going there as *Madam Butterfly* was to be performed. We were delighted, and at the right time he drove us to the theatre. I had heard *Madam Butterfly* heaps of times in England, but in Iceland it was surely something special. To begin with, Butterfly, the Japanese heroine, was a celebrated Swedish soprano. Pinkerton, a fine Icelandic tenor who was once a butcher, had trained in Italy. The handsome baritone, whose name I forget was equally splendid, and so too was the chorus who mainly consisted of housewives, shop assistants and so forth. All sang beautifully. The costumes and stage designs could not have been surpassed – not even at Covent Garden. It was, I think, the most enchanting rendering of this much-loved opera that I have ever heard. Especially shall I remember forever the "Humming Chorus" that has no words, and needs none. As I write of it now a little quivering strain of the music tugs my heart.

I have finished writing about those halcyon days, although to me they might have been only yesterday. For some reason they have always been exclusively their own, and the sweet sorrow of distance makes it even sweeter.

As I look at the gracious bracelet around my arm I am ever reminded of the day when Audur took me into a jeweller's shop in Reykjavik. She there begged me to try on the bracelet I liked best. I had no idea that it was meant for me, for we both tried on various trinkets. Eventually I tried on this wide silver-gilt Icelandic filigree bracelet.

"Isn't this beautiful," I said, gazing down at it in wonder.

"Do you really like it?" said Audur. "I'll have a safety chain put on the clasp. It's for you from Halldór and me, in remembrance." And so on my right wrist my cherished Icelandic bracelet always surrounds it while on my left wrist is the twisted golden chain with its tiny gold cross hanging from it.

The day arrived. I travelled with two cousins of Audur, so the flight seemed shorter, and I never tired of hearing about Iceland from them, and of the strangeness of its graphic landscape. We parted at the airport, and during their four weeks' stay in London (which they knew well) they came to my studio several times. It was sad to bid farewell once more as their plane flew high, almost like a ghost moving into the atmosphere and on to their Arctic homeland.

CHAPTER 17

RECENTLY I heard the words, "He careth for you". Although I know those words are perfectly true I also find them difficult to believe at times. That spiritual torment gets the better of me and I somehow expect immediate answers to my prayers. Yet if I wait confidently, God answers me in a still small voice, and He tells me all I need. The actual voice I never hear, but if I listen quietly and carefully, His voice breathes through my innermost being. And so it came to me last autumn. I happened to meet my BBC producer who was walking near the Headquarters as I was going that way. I remember that it was pouring with rain and he invited me in to shelter and to have something to eat. Our conversation turned to talks. I had not given one for three years. Why had I not written one, he enquired? I told him that on the whole I led an extremely quiet life, and that I painted and tried to write, but ill health had prevented me from doing so quite often. As we talked he suggested that I should write a talk about the things in my studio and that I should send it to him.

The creative impulse responded immediately, and when I returned home I glanced around the studio. There were plenty of objects, apart from pictures, and so I decided that I would try to bring them together, and do my best to write about them. None of the objects was of any particular value apart from certain paintings, but they had all been given to me or brought by friends from abroad, and I treasured them. I had to think of the fifteen minutes that were allotted for my talk. Should I ever be able to write sufficient words to last for a quarter of an hour? But I did manage – in fact I wrote far too many words and we had to eliminate some of them.

I loved thinking out the script, however difficult it was, and to expanding the sentences from single words about the objects and the joy they have always given me. I remembered the very first talk. It was then more difficult for me to speak properly, and my producer and I went over the script for two hours beforehand. Eventually I was able to compose myself, and the actual recording was made. Even then some of the sentences and words had to be recorded over and over again. This time, however, my speech was much better, and only a few things had to be recorded two or three times over. My producer had told me that I should not keep rehearsing the talk at home. But I said that if I did not do that he would certainly never give me another date, for I would be stumbling all along, mainly from nervousness. I wanted to be a credit to him, and also to my consultant and my Rector without whom I should be lost in a void of helplessness. I asked the producer whether I might make the record early one morning, as I felt much fresher at that time of the day. So it was agreed.

After three years I saw that things had not changed much in the BBC, and studios are very similar for talks. Putting the little things I might need beside me on the table, I began. For a few seconds I felt like a stranger who was peering over a new script. In my thoughts I was far away from what I was supposed to be reading. I was asked to begin again and to think of what I was doing! It was not easy to get accustomed to broadcasting once more. Recording on one's own seems somehow unreal when one is actually reading the script. At last the red bulb flashed and I counted the ten seconds intently. It was now time to begin. Once or twice I hesitated or stumbled, and my producer came forth from his glass-like case and corrected my words or sentences. Those fifteen minutes seemed never-ending.

Suddenly it was all over. The red light flickered out and I sat back and relaxed. As I finished the coffee someone had kindly put beside me, my producer again appeared. I said to him, "Was it awful?"

He laughed cheerfully and replied: "No, you pulled it off." I could hardly believe my ears, but as my producer is very strict regarding things being as good as possible, I felt pleased. Actually I had no idea that the talk needed "pulling off" after the nerve-racking rehearsal (on my part), so I was rather glad, otherwise I doubt whether I would ever have been able to "pull it off" naturally! The contents of the script were very simple, but in my eyes they had always been luminated by magic.

As I walked down Oxford Street I was already thinking about the next talk, although it wasn't quite as easy as that. Still, I had made another start, and many ideas now flashed through my mind. I was terribly hampered by being unable to walk too far, and far more difficult than that—to be able to think clearly and quickly. My mind became dizzier than ever when I thought hard, and my legs had difficulty in walking straight, for I had no technical aids. My stick, though solid, would leave me at any moment as it sometimes does, and I would fall over it. All the same Jesus, my beloved friend, gets me through most untold scrapes, and often I talk to Him silently as I walk along.

My little boat is sailing still, although at one time I thought it was safely in harbour. And at other times those waves are greatly agitated and I am afraid they will swamp me. If only the boat and I might sail into tideless waters for a change, and find harmony once more! I take out the little book which has a daily message from Him, and I look at what it says today. Today the words are from Jesus Himself. He says, "Fear thou not, for I am with thee." Then I close the book and say a little prayer. I look at the waves again. They appear just as sweeping and windswept as ever, but my befogged eyes suddenly notice a slight difference in the horizon, and I know that my long heart-breaking vigil is ending. The shadow that once deepened the air is now graced with sunlight. Did not God say, "Fear thou not for I am with thee"? I often think of my little boat as I walk along although now I am more often on land than on the sea.

After the last broadcast, which apparently was a success, my producer suggested that I should try to write about the pictures in my studio. Furthermore, pictures were my initial occupation, as well as being the springboard of my livelihood. And I dearly loved them. So I said I would try. Various sorts of pictures hang or lean against something in the studio. There's a story about most of them, and as I looked at each one it seemed to speak to me in undertones. Some held sad memories although they were brilliantly imaginative, while others gave me shining glances without uttering a single word. And into the bargain they indicated their warm friendship, inviting me to rest in their companionship. That was the world where once I had spent most of my life.

In these silent recollections I enjoyed writing the script, even though, like everything else I tried to write, it took me a long time to do. My producer liked it, and in June 1967 I recorded it and it was broadcast later in the month. The thought of giving two broadcasts fairly closely to one another gave me a lot of joy. I was trying to get away from the cerebral haemorrhage although of course I knew that I could never do that, try as I might. They have been treacherous in numerous ways, but Jesus has helped me all along, and when I am particularly desperate His quiet soundless voice comes to my rescue.

My letter box, as I have said, has always been a most captivating object in my estimation. It has its ups and downs, for not all the letters that are pushed through its wide mouth are pleasant ones. I was awake early (as I thought) when I heard the postman pushing something through the letter box. I jumped out of bed and flew to see what was there. The gentle handwriting on the envelope I knew well, but when I opened it I could scarcely believe my eyes. This particular consultant whom I had known for years, but who through illness had been forced to leave London, had gone with his family to live in Troon. Would I like to go and stay with them. Would I? The thought of it was dazzling. Most of the previous year had been thwarted with illness or recovering from it, or the shock of that previous letter I was not expecting. I knew that Jesus was always beside me when I sought Him. He was my true friend, yet sometimes in desperation I felt He had hidden behind the passing clouds. It was taking me a long time to preserve the appearance of real happiness although at times I really possessed it. So when I picked up the letter on the mat the atmosphere completely changed. It was almost like returning to Iceland. There were so many things to think about, and I knew that the long train journey to Scotland would be out of the question. I knew, too, from their letters, that their house looked over the sea, and that the garden almost ran down to the sand dunes, and from thence to the sea. How wonderful it must be, I imagined!

My Rector was delighted with the idea and so was my consultant (who had in 1966 become a Professor). We discussed it—excitedly on my part—and it was left to me to make arrangements. My head seemed like pandemonium as I tried to sort out the various problems. Between our letters from Troon to Apple Tree Studio and from the studio to Troon, the arrangements were crystallized. I was to fly in a BEA plane and my friends would meet me there. I had thought that I would never fly again after my return from Iceland over two years ago, and yet there I was having had a near third stroke, and later a paralysed back (all in one year) and soon flying to Scotland. Friends had been wonderfully kind.

In this instance I was hardly afraid of flying. It took only an hour, and the delicious meal took most of the time. I enjoyed almost every moment of it. The smooth flight without any air bumps made me feel as though I were now a seasoned traveller. At the bottom of the steps of the airport there stood my friends scattering kindness to me in every direction, and Troon had certainly bestowed on them its lovely brown tan. After having been there for a few days I, too, knew its quickening air. For me the level of the town and sands were perfect, and I did not have to use my stick at all. I practically lived on the beach apart from meal times, and my friends who knew my love of simple things left me to do what I liked. The house, as they had told me, overlooked the sea, and the seascape and sky, even from the big windows, were a source of infinite beauty. As for the shells on the beach, well, I can only say that I was in my seventh heaven, picking them up and collecting them in a plastic bag to bring home with me. My friends were just as addicted to shells as I was, and at times they went with me. They were able to bathe from the house. It was but a few steps from the garden to the dunes and from thence on to the sands and into the sea. Oh, how inviting it was, but I knew my limitations. If I wandered a short way into its wizardly depths and looked down, I knew that my head would swim and not myself, and I should lose consciousness and sink under those gentle waves. So I just paddled on the edge and did not bend my head unless I were out of it.

I have decided to give my Troon shells an entire chapter all to themselves. They are so pregnant with imagery that as I look at them in my studio their evocations remind me of those lazy summer days and the happiness I found there.

CHAPTER 18

As long as I can remember I have kept small tins of shells lying about in my room. I even found one recently hidden at the back of a drawer. The shells were always put in lozenge tins because the lids were completely secure. Most of the shells were small, but I loved them desperately, and I have never grown tired of that love. I often think of the gentle poem by Tennyson, and a verse of it runs like this:

> *See what a lovely shell*
> *Small and pure as a pearl,*
> *Lying close to my foot,*
> *Frail, but a work divine,*
> *Made so fairly well,*
> *With delicate spire and whorl,*
> *How exquisitely minute*
> *A miracle of design.*

So when I look at my shells (and my studio is full of them) I think of that poem in particular. Many of them came back from Troon together with various pieces of seaweed, all in plastic bags. I look at the miraculous colours and patterns that no human hand could ever design or make. They are as precious to me as a newly found flower by the wayside, and I marvel at the handicraft of His creative genius.

When I returned from Troon I did quite a lot of research on British shells, and the more I gaze at my own shells around me the more wonderful they seem to me. Each one has been washed over and swept by the sea on to its sandy resting place. How many people notice them as they pass by these days? This is not an age of eulogising such simple things. Yet as I used to look through my bedroom window in the early morning I studied the shining beach waiting for me outside. The trembling golden mist there was not quite ready to disclose its full glory. So I watched. The long beach at that time of the morning was usually rather deserted, and I knew that when I zig-zagged there, over the sand dunes, I would find endless joy at the simple treasures around my feet. Each day was full of them. They were gifts from God, and those of us who love Him, as well as the magical surprises He gives us, are conscious and humbly grateful for His tenderness and love. Some times I felt rather like a voyager treading softly in another world.

Many of the commoner shells I liked best, particularly the small oblong Sunset shells. They were exquisite. Their rays of concentric lines of various colours were so delicate that they almost wrung my heart for their sheer beauty. It was easy to understand why they were so named. When I first saw the beach I knew perfectly well that I would never be able to resist the lovely charms those quivering sands held for me. Once a friend put a bag of tiny miraculous pink shells in a big common mussel shell, together with other minute seashore lore that had stuck themselves together. The entire manifestation looked rather like some precious object in a jeweller's glass case. Occasionally I found a double Sunset shell that was entirely closed, so I imagined that the little creature was still inside, and I threw it back into the sea. Others that were still hinged had opened, and the occupants had gone leaving their shell reflections that somehow looked like wings. They were so frail. The Venus shells I brought back in my plastic bag were much tougher than the Sunsets, and they were not at all polished. I look so often at this medley of shells when I dust them, and I remember with what rapture I picked them up. The Venus shells were shaped like rounded triangles in various tones of leaf green and autumn yellow touched with white. I have heard them called "heart-shaped". Their sculptured frills at the bottom of their shells were fluted. They were so pretty and harmonious. I thought they almost looked as though they had been woven on a loom.

Sometimes when I was walking along the beach I would just stand there looking at those encrustations on stones, and occasionally on shells as well. The sea shore is fascinating to such as myself. It bewitches me, and in a way it acts as a kind of tranquilliser. I would lie among the sand dunes hardly conscious that I was lying on this earth, so idyllic was everything. Usually I was barefooted, and I loved the feeling of the sinuous sands beneath my feet. I never fell over once nor did I have the feeling of dizziness. It was just as though an Unseen Power was always protecting me. I must have walked endlessly with my leisurely pace on the damp beach—or even into the sea for a second or two without realising it! Eventually I would retrace my steps and find rest in the shade of the sand dune grasses. There I lay and gazed around the wide bay and the hazy hills beyond. A Latin quotation often flashed through my mind. It said something about "the tears in things". That was perfectly true. Whatever God makes seems to have divine elation of humility and tears.

I could go on writing about shells indefinitely, but not everyone else is as engrossed in them as myself. In fact I know very few people who adore them as much as I do, both as an artist and an ascetic. Many of the shells have delicious names and I can never understand why some folk like to paint their shells in different colours. They even emboss them! To me they are absolutely perfect as they are, distilling the sweetest essences of their origin.

One thing more I would like to add, and that is the appealing little pools that appeared on my sandy walks. Often I would peer down into their limited depths. They completely hypnotised me. The bottom of most of these pools were covered with shells and stones. Around the edges of them emerald green seaweed fringed the tops, and the bright wet surfaces displayed their charms below. That was something I shall never forget, nor indeed the ephemeral wings of time that just vanished. Those magical moments now console me, as I lift up an almost transparent piece of feathery pink seaweed. The sun-warmed grace retains its retentive sea perfume as I lay it down in a bowl, along with other sea lore. Wordsworth once defined a lyric as "emotion recollected in tranquillity". One does not need a lyric to recollect a sensitive affection for its subject. My subjects are always before me in one or another part of the studio. Their subtle graces breathe enchantment to me as well as the warmth of friendship that hovers around them.

CHAPTER 19

NEVER had I felt so well for a long time since my holiday at Troon. I did not immediately begin to write or paint, although the urge to write was beginning to weave its cocoon around my brain. The summer had been so glorious that I wanted to take advantage of its loveliness. Besides, the thought of living in a great city, with all its whirlwind of traffic and formidabilities seemed to hold no part for me. The galleries always attracted me, as they did when I was able to write about them, and their press cards still follow me. How I longed to be able to write for an editor who could understand my handicap and give me a little time to think out an article now and them. However, it was no use moaning. God understood my secret sorrow, and the dizzy damaged brain that was so elusive, and sometimes moribund. I tried to paint after nearly a year, but I seemed to make a mess of everything I did, and in any case my heart was not in it.

I felt so much that I would like to help those who have the same complaint as my own. It needs patience – much patience, but I believe I have that, although I am not a physiotherapist. Three times I took out my paints and paper and put big sheets of newspaper on my table so that I could lay my piece of rice paper on it. After many attempts of thinking about the heavenly sunsets at Troon I managed to "pull one off". This was better than I imagined. It was quite small, and I had tried to put into the sunset colour the healing that lay behind it. The sky and the sunset were reflected in the sea. I thought of the little verse so often:

> Oh Lord, protect me;
> Thy sea is so wide,
> My boat is so small.

After I'd finished the sunset I tried to paint another one,

but it was quite hopeless. God had certainly helped me with this one and now He wanted me to continue on my own. Alas, I could not do so. The creative urge had dropped a veil before my eyes, so I tried to be content with what I had done. I threw away endless sheets, one after another, until I was beginning to wonder what my next move should be. The summer was still warm and golden. I looked at my paint boxes and decided to put them away for the time being. The evocative Troon holiday had given me much to think about, for it was just as perfect as my last Icelandic trip, although in a different way.

By now you will know that my letter box has practically become human to me. It is the most provocative object I have because it can be coy, sinister, beckoning, forlorn and delightful. In the following instance I had just eaten my breakfast and I was about to clear it away when I thought I would glance to see whether the letter box had dropped down anything for me. Indeed it had! The strong black handwriting did not often come my way, but when it did it was always heart-warming. In the letter, which was as always written in black ink, the sender told me that she had been living in South America for the last ten years. During one of her summer trips to England she had fallen in love with a fifteenth-century cottage in Gloucestershire and had bought it. She had had it repaired, and would I go to stay with her? Again my problems had been solved. Our interchanged letters arranged dates, and before long my friend met me at the station of memories.

We drove some distance into the heart of the country. It was ravishing. There was no pressure of traffic either before or behind. No tenseness or sense of time. Looking around, everything and everywhere really did seem timeless. We turned the many graceful corners of the lanes like dancers on wheels. Overhead the lacy leaves of the trees on either side gave the light a chance to filter through. Driving along a narrow lane we then drove through two fields, and there, at the bottom of the last one we arrived at the cottage. It was absolutely remote and certainly far, far from the maddening crowd.

The beautiful fifteenth-century cottage overlooked one of the most glorious valleys in Gloucestershire. As I lay in bed I used to look at the huge beams overhead, and I listened to the irresistible chorus of the bleating lambs in the field below my window. I did not truly feel like painting or writing, although there was every opportunity to do so. I was quite glad that there was no radio, TV or newspapers, and of course no shops for miles. My friend, who is an artist, had a studio in another part of the grounds, and the landscape through the large window reflected the trouble-free world that I, for one, seldom see. It seemed unreal to think that I had come from the earth-bound world of savage reality into the dazzling enchantment of nature. A stream trickled along below the slope of a hillside nearby and I had to pinch myself to make sure that the fluttering cloak of nature was solid, too, even though it was never really quite still. God's handiwork took my breath away, and here again I was perfectly content to gaze at the smiling landscape that surrounded me.

Only one thing worried me. In Troon most things were more or less on the level, whereas in this part of the country, although it was delightful to look at, it was bad for my legs. My walks mainly seemed to be made up of hillocks, and that made me feel abnormally dizzy. I could not have believed that bounteous countryside with its continual uphills and downhills, even for short walks, lightly shadowed most of my joys in these slight exertions. I had always loved the explosive countryside that was mingled with feckless magic. Now I realised that even though I tried to walk with straight and lighthearted steps, inwardly they were uncertain and restrained, and I had to be careful in case I might fall over . . . that is, until I returned to London when my gaze was lost in my thoughts. The delicious smell of tall grasses and visions of streams and flowers and trees would suddenly plunge through my being and I would know that "God's in His heaven, all's right with the world".

CHAPTER 20

IT was more difficult than ever to settle down in my studio after such wonderful holidays by the sea and in the country. Yet my anchorage to the studio has always held me to it, and I have clung tenaciously to its load of sorrows spiced with happiness. Within these walls I have gradually learned some of the words and meanings of Jesus Christ. I know, too, how much they mean to me. Without them I could not possibly exist. He is indispensable to such as myself who could so easily live on wishful day-dreams. I love Him with all my heart. He is my dearest friend. The feeling of abandonment that sometimes attacks me suddenly gives my sobbing words that blessed quietitude and I hear His still small voice breathing through the quintessence of my being. "I will never leave thee, nor forsake thee," He says.

During the years I have found what Holy Communion means to me. I thought I knew, but at one time I had not been able to think for more than a second or two. Now I am able to concentrate for a few seconds longer. A scatty, damaged brain cannot always reflect on what it listens to, nor indeed on what it reads, try though it may.

St. Peter's, a small and beautiful church belonging to All Souls', holds a Communion service weekly, and I try to go. There are fewer people, and somehow I feel better able to concentrate. During these Holy Communion services I have truly become aware of what our Lord Jesus Christ did for us all, and how He was crucified on the cross for our sins. It has taken a long, long time for me to realise this thoroughly – I mean, in my deepest depths – and to know how He must have felt in His mortal agony. I am so grateful to be able to listen to the tender service there.

Since I began this book several years have elapsed. I am older now than I was then, although age has never meant anything in particular to me. Still, it was harder for me to cope with life then than it is now. There are things that I know I cannot do, nor will ever be able to do, so I just leave them alone and try not to burst with grief. On the whole my thoughts are not easy to formulate, nor to put together in a sentence that can be easily written. The grey wastes of space close in on my brain, and like ragged clouds they are often laden with sorrows. My Word Book is ever beside me as I write, yet sometimes when I feverishly turn the pages they look full of nothing but emptiness. At the beginning of the book I had already torn pages in it. Now they are worse than ever, and so, too, is the shabby binding. But I ignore all that. Once upon a time I had thought of tearing it into little pieces, thinking that, like myself, it was meant only for the shadows. But faith, that wonderful word that holds us in its inexplicable care can triumph over the sadness and heart-breaks of this world.

In the beginning of the first half of this book I recalled then only a pale recollection of His goodness to me; yet unhesitatingly I yielded to His outstretched hands and silently accepted His love. And shining through the darkness of that night in the ward when I was able to murmur just two words—"Our Father"—I now hear His soundless voice breathing in my ear: "I am the Good Shepherd; the Good Shepherd giveth his life for the sheep. My sheep hear My voice, and I know them and they follow Me."